Praise for the Patrick Melrose novels

'Clearly one of the major achievements of contemporary British fiction. Stingingly well-written and exhilaratingly funny' David Sexton, *Evening Standard*

'From the very first lines I was completely hooked . . . By turns witty, moving and an intense social comedy, I wept at the end but wouldn't dream of giving away the totally unexpected reason' Antonia Fraser, *Sunday Telegraph*

'Wonderful caustic wit . . . Perhaps the very sprightliness of the prose – its lapidary concision and moral certitude – represents the cure for which the characters yearn. So much good writing is in itself a form of health'
Edmund White, *Guardian*

'The Patrick Melrose novels can be read as the navigational charts of a mariner desperate not to end up in the wretched harbor from which he embarked on a voyage that has led in and out of heroin addiction, alcoholism, marital infidelity and a range of behaviors for which the term "self-destructive" is the mildest of euphemisms. Some of the most perceptive, elegantly written and hilarious novels of our era . . . Remarkable' Francine Prose, *New York Times*

'Perhaps the most brilliant English novelist of his generation'
Alan Hollinghurst

'Beautifully written, excruciatingly funny and also very tragic' Mariella Frostrup, *Sky Magazine*

'The main joy of a St Aubyn novel is the exquisite clarity of his prose, the almost uncanny sense he gives that, in language as in mathematical formulae, precision and beauty invariably point to truth . . . Characters in St Aubyn novels are hyper-articulate, and the witty dialogue is here, as ever, one of the chief joys' Suzi Feay, *Financial Times*

'Humor, pathos, razor-sharp judgement, pain, joy and everything in between. The Melrose novels are a masterwork for the twenty-first century, by one of our greatest prose stylists'
Alice Sebold

'Edward St Aubyn, like Proust, has created a world in which no one in their right mind would like to live but which feels real and vivid and hilariously and dangerously vacuous. Who better than he to turn to if your faith in the future of literary fiction is wavering?' Alan Taylor, *Herald*

'The act of investigative self-repair has all along been the underlying project of these extraordinary novels. It is the source of their urgent emotional intensity, and the determining principle of their construction. For all their brilliant social satire, they are closer to the tight, ritualistic poetic drama of another era than the expansive comic fiction of our own . . . A terrifying, spectacularly entertaining saga'
James Lasdun, *Guardian*

'The wit of Wilde, the lightness of Wodehouse and the waspishness of Waugh. A joy' Zadie Smith, *Harpers*

'A masterpiece. Edward St Aubyn is a writer of immense gifts' Patrick McGrath

'Irony courses through these pages like adrenaline . . . Patrick's intelligence processes his predicaments into elegant, lucid, dispassionate, near-aphoristic formulations . . . Brimming with witty flair, sardonic perceptiveness and literary finesse' Peter Kemp, *Sunday Times*

'His prose has an easy charm that masks a ferocious, searching intellect. As a sketcher of character, his wit – whether turned against pointless members of the aristocracy or hopeless crack dealers – is ticklingly wicked. As an analyser of broken minds and tired hearts he is as energetic, careful and creative as the perfect shrink. And when it comes to spinning a good yarn, whether over the grand scale or within a single page of anecdote, he has a natural talent for keeping you on the edge of your seat' Melissa Katsoulis, *The Times*

'In the end, it is language that provides Patrick – and St Aubyn – with consolation . . . St Aubyn's Melrose novels now deserve to be thought of as an important roman-fleuve'
Henry Hitchings, *Times Literary Supplement*

'Blackly comic, superbly written fiction . . . His style is crisp and light; his similes exhilarating in their accuracy . . . St Aubyn writes with luminous tenderness of Patrick's love for his sons' Caroline Moore, *Sunday Telegraph*

'St Aubyn conveys the chaos of emotion, the confusion of heightened sensation, and the daunting contradictions of intellectual endeavour with a force and subtlety that have an exhilarating, almost therapeutic effect'
Francis Wyndham, *New York Review of Books*

'The darkest possible comedy about the cruelty of the old to the young, vicious and excruciatingly honest. It opened my eyes to a whole realm of experience I have never seen written about. That's the mark of a masterpiece' *The Times*

'Edward St Aubyn has transformed his appalling childhood into something dazzling and disturbing. A brilliant satire' *Psychologies Magazine*

'St Aubyn is a genuinely creative writer rather than a peddler of misery memoirs and so his elegant, sardonic and often very funny books transcend whatever circumstances led to their making . . . His prose is a pleasure to read and his insights can be as telling as they're funny. And forgiving, too' *Irish Independent*

'I've loved Edward St Aubyn's Patrick Melrose novels. Read them all, now' David Nicholls

'A humane meditation on lives blighted by the sins of the previous generation. St Aubyn remains among the cream of British novelists' *Sunday Times*

'The sharpest and best series since Anthony Powell's *A Dance to the Music of Time*. St Aubyn dances on the thin ice of modern upper-class manners, the pain of displaced emotions and the hope of happiness' *Saga Magazine*

'St Aubyn puts an entire family under a microscope, laying bare all its painful, unavoidable complexities. At once epic and intimate, appalling and comic, the novels are masterpieces, each and every one' Maggie O'Farrell

Some Hope

Edward St Aubyn was born in London in 1960. His superbly acclaimed Patrick Melrose novels are *Never Mind*, *Bad News*, *Some Hope* (previously published collectively as the *Some Hope* trilogy), *Mother's Milk* (shortlisted for the Man Booker Prize 2006) and *At Last*. He is also the author of the novels *A Clue to the Exit* and *On the Edge*.

Also by Edward St Aubyn

The Patrick Melrose novels

NEVER MIND

BAD NEWS

MOTHER'S MILK

AT LAST

ON THE EDGE

A CLUE TO THE EXIT

EDWARD ST AUBYN

SOME HOPE

PICADOR

First published 1994 by William Heinemann

First published in paperback 1998 as part of
The Patrick Melrose Trilogy by Vintage

First published by Picador in paperback 2007 as part of
Some Hope: A Trilogy

This edition published 2012 by Picador
an imprint of Pan Macmillan, a division of Macmillan Publishers Limited
Pan Macmillan, 20 New Wharf Road, London N1 9RR
Basingstoke and Oxford
Associated companies throughout the world
www.panmacmillan.com

ISBN 978-1-4472-0296-7

7 9 8

A CIP catalogue record for this book is available from
the British Library.

Typeset by Intype Libra Ltd
Printed and bound by CPI Group (UK) Ltd, Croydon, CR0 4YY

For my mother, and my sister

SOME HOPE

1

Patrick woke up knowing he had dreamed but unable to remember the contents of his dream. He felt the familiar ache of trying to track something that had just disappeared off the edge of consciousness but could still be inferred from its absence, like a whirlwind of scrap paper left by the passage of a fast car.

The obscure fragments of his dream, which seemed to have taken place beside a lake, were confused with the production of *Measure for Measure* he had seen the night before with Johnny Hall. Despite the director's choice of a bus depot as the setting for the play, nothing could diminish the shock of hearing the word 'mercy' so many times in one evening.

Perhaps all his problems arose from using the wrong vocabulary, he thought, with a brief flush of excitement that enabled him to throw aside the bedcovers and contemplate getting up. He moved in a world in which the word 'charity', like a beautiful woman shadowed by her jealous husband, was invariably qualified by the words 'lunch', 'committee', or 'ball'. 'Compassion' nobody had any time for, whereas 'leniency' made frequent appearances in the form of complaints about short prison sentences. Still, he knew that his difficulties were more fundamental than that.

He was worn out by his lifelong need to be in two places at once: in his body and out of his body, on the bed and on the curtain pole, in the vein and in the barrel, one eye behind the eyepatch and one eye looking at the eyepatch, trying to stop observing by becoming unconscious, and then forced to observe the fringes of unconsciousness and make darkness visible; cancelling every effort, but spoiling apathy with restlessness; drawn to puns but repelled by the virus of ambiguity; inclined to divide sentences in half, pivoting them on the qualification of a 'but', but longing to unwind his coiled tongue like a gecko's and catch a distant fly with unwavering skill; desperate to escape the self-subversion of irony and say what he really meant, but really meaning what only irony could convey.

Not to mention, thought Patrick, as he swung his feet out of bed, the two places he wanted to be tonight: at Bridget's party and *not* at Bridget's party. And he wasn't in the mood to dine with people called Bossington-Lane. He would ring Johnny and arrange to have dinner with him alone. He dialled the number but immediately hung up, deciding to call again after he had made some tea. He had scarcely replaced the receiver when the phone rang. Nicholas Pratt was ringing to chastise him for not answering his invitation to Cheatley.

'No need to thank me,' said Nicholas Pratt, 'for getting you invited to this glittering occasion tonight. I owe it to your dear Papa to see that you get into the swim of things.'

'I'm drowning in it,' said Patrick. 'Anyhow, you prepared the way for my invitation to Cheatley by bringing Bridget down to Lacoste when I was five. Even then one could tell she was destined to command the heights of society.'

'You were much too badly behaved to notice anything as important as *that*,' said Nicholas. 'I remember you once in Victoria Road giving me a very sharp kick in the shins. I hobbled through the hall, trying to hide my agony so as not to upset your sainted mother. How is she, by the way? One never sees her these days.'

'It's amazing, isn't it? She seems to think there are better things to do than going to parties.'

'I always thought she was a little peculiar,' said Nicholas wisely.

'As far as I know she's driving a consignment of ten thousand syringes to Poland. People say it's marvellous of her, but I still think that charity begins at home. She could have saved herself the journey by bringing them round to my flat,' said Patrick.

'I thought you'd put all that behind you,' said Nicholas.

'Behind me, in front of me. It's hard to tell, here in the Grey Zone.'

'That's rather a melodramatic way to talk at thirty.'

'Well, you see,' sighed Patrick, 'I've given up everything, but taken nothing up instead.'

'You could make a start by taking my daughter up to Cheatley.'

'I'm afraid I can't,' lied Patrick, who couldn't bear Amanda Pratt. 'I'm getting a lift from someone else.'

'Oh, well, you'll see her at the Bossington-Lanes',' said Nicholas. 'And we'll see each other at the party.'

Patrick had been reluctant to accept his invitation

to Cheatley for several reasons. One was that Debbie was going to be there. After years of trying to thrust her away, he was bewildered by his sudden success. She, on the other hand, seemed to enjoy falling out of love with him more than anything else about their long affair. How could he blame her? He ached with unspoken apologies.

In the eight years since his father's death, Patrick's youth had slipped away without being replaced by any signs of maturity, unless the tendency for sadness and exhaustion to eclipse hatred and insanity could be called 'mature'. The sense of multiplying alternatives and bifurcating paths had been replaced by a quay-side desolation, contemplating the long list of missed boats. He had been weaned from his drug addiction in several clinics, leaving promiscuity and party-going to soldier on uncertainly, like troops which have lost their commander. His money, eroded by extravagance and medical bills, kept him from poverty without enabling him to buy his way out of boredom. Quite recently, to his horror, he had realized he would have to get a job. He was therefore studying to become a barrister, in the hope that he would find some pleasure in keeping as many criminals as possible at large.

His decision to study the law had got him as far

as hiring *Twelve Angry Men* from a video shop. He had spent several days pacing up and down, demolishing imaginary witnesses with withering remarks, or suddenly leaning on furniture and saying with mounting contempt, 'I put it to you that on the night of . . .' until he recoiled, and, turning into the victim of his own cross-examination, collapsed in a fit of histrionic sobs. He had also bought some books, like *The Concept of Law*, *Street on Tort*, and *Charlesworth on Negligence*, and this pile of law books now competed for his attention with old favourites like *Twilight of the Idols* and *The Myth of Sisyphus*.

As the drugs had worn off, a couple of years earlier, he had started to realize what it must be like to be lucid all the time, an unpunctuated stretch of consciousness, a white tunnel, hollow and dim, like a bone with the marrow sucked out. 'I want to die, I want to die, I want to die,' he found himself muttering in the middle of the most ordinary task, swept away by a landslide of regret as the kettle boiled or the toast popped up.

At the same time, his past lay before him like a corpse waiting to be embalmed. He was woken every night by savage nightmares; too frightened to sleep, he climbed out of his sweat-soaked sheets and smoked cigarettes until the dawn crept into the sky, pale and dirty as the gills of a poisonous mushroom. His flat in Ennismore Gardens was strewn with violent videos which were a shadowy expression of the endless reel of violence that played in his head. Constantly on the verge of hallucination, he walked on ground that undulated softly, like a swallowing throat.

Worst of all, as his struggle against drugs grew more successful, he saw how it had masked a struggle not to become like his father. The claim that every man kills the thing he loves seemed to him a wild guess compared with the near certainty of a man turning into the thing he hates. There were of course people who didn't hate anything, but they were too remote from Patrick for him to imagine their fate. The memory of his father still hypnotized him and drew him like a sleepwalker towards a precipice of unwilling emulation. Sarcasm, snobbery, cruelty, and betrayal seemed less nauseating than the terrors that brought them into existence. What could he do but become a machine for turning terror into contempt? How could he relax his guard when beams of neurotic energy, like searchlights weaving about a prison compound, allowed no thought to escape, no remark to go unchecked.

The pursuit of sex, the fascination with one body or another, the little rush of an orgasm, so much feebler and more laborious than the rush of drugs, but like an injection, constantly repeated because its role was essentially palliative – all this was compulsive enough, but its social complications were paramount: the treachery, the danger of pregnancy, of infection, of discovery, the pleasures of theft, the tensions that arose in what might otherwise have been very tedious circumstances; and the way that sex merged with the penetration of ever more self-assured social circles where, perhaps, he would find a resting place, a living equivalent to the intimacy and reassurance offered by the octopus embrace of narcotics.

As Patrick reached for his cigarettes, the phone rang again.

'So, how are you?' said Johnny.

'I'm stuck in one of those argumentative daydreams,' said Patrick. 'I don't know why I think intelligence consists of proving that I can have a row all on my own, but it would be nice just to grasp something for a change.'

'*Measure for Measure* is a very argumentative play,' said Johnny.

'I know,' said Patrick. 'I ended up theoretically

accepting that people have to forgive on a "judge not that ye be not judged" basis, but there isn't any emotional authority for it, at least not in that play.'

'Exactly,' said Johnny. 'If behaving badly was a good enough reason to forgive bad behaviour, we'd all be oozing with magnanimity.'

'But what is a good enough reason?' asked Patrick.

'Search me. I'm more and more convinced that things just happen, or don't just happen, and there's not much you can do to hurry them along.' Johnny had only just thought of this idea and was not convinced of it at all.

'Ripeness is all,' groaned Patrick.

'Yes, exactly, another play altogether,' said Johnny.

'It's important to decide which play you're in before you get out of bed,' said Patrick.

'I don't think anyone's heard of the one we're in tonight. Who are the Bossington-Lanes?'

'Are they having you for dinner too?' asked Patrick. 'I think we're going to have to break down on the motorway, don't you? Have dinner in the hotel. It's so hard facing strangers without drugs.'

Patrick and Johnny, although they now fed on grilled food and mineral water, had a well-established nostalgia for their former existence.

'But when we took gear at parties, all we saw was the inside of the loos,' Johnny pointed out.

'I know,' said Patrick. 'Nowadays when I go into the loos I say to myself, "What are you doing here? You don't take drugs anymore!" It's only after I've stormed out that I realize I wanted to have a piss. By the way, shall we drive down to Cheatley together?'

'Sure, but I have to go to an NA meeting at three o'clock.'

'I don't know how you put up with those meetings,' said Patrick. 'Aren't they full of ghastly people?'

'Of course they are, but so is any crowded room,' said Johnny.

'But at least I'm not required to believe in God to go to this party tonight.'

'I'm sure if you were you'd find a way,' laughed Johnny. 'What is a strain is being forced into the lobster pot of good behaviour while being forced to sing its praises.'

'Doesn't the hypocrisy get you down?'

'Luckily, they have a slogan for that: "Fake it to make it."'

Patrick made a vomiting sound. 'I don't think that dressing the Ancient Mariner as a wedding guest is the solution to the problem, do you?'

'It's not like that, more like a roomful of Ancient Mariners deciding to have a party of their own.'

'Christ!' said Patrick. 'It's worse than I thought.'

'You're the one who wants to dress as a wedding guest,' said Johnny. 'Didn't you tell me that the last time you were banging your head against the wall and begging to be released from the torment of your addiction, you couldn't get that sentence about Henry James out of your mind: "He was an inveterate diner-out and admitted to accepting one hundred and fifty invitations in the winter of 1878," or something like that?'

'Hmm,' said Patrick.

'Anyhow, don't you find it hard not to take drugs?' asked Johnny.

'Of course it's hard, it's a fucking nightmare,' said Patrick. Since he was representing stoicism against therapy, he wasn't going to lose the chance to exaggerate the strain he was under.

'Either I wake up in the Grey Zone,' he whispered, 'and I've forgotten how to breathe, and my feet are so far away I'm not sure I can afford the air fare; or it's the endless reel of lazy decapitations, and kneecaps stolen by passing traffic, and dogs fighting over the liver I quite want back. If they made a film of my inner life, it would be more than the public could take. Mothers would scream, “Bring back *The Texas Chainsaw Massacre*, so we can have some decent family entertainment!” And all these joys accompanied by the fear that I’ll forget everything that’s ever happened to me, and all the things I’ve seen will be lost, as the Replicant says at the end of *Blade Runner*, “like tears in rain”.’

‘Yeah, yeah,’ said Johnny, who’d often heard Patrick rehearse fragments of this speech. ‘So why don’t you just go ahead?’

‘Some combination of pride and terror,’ said Patrick, and then, changing the subject quickly, he asked when Johnny’s meeting ended. They agreed to leave from Patrick’s flat at five o’clock.

Patrick lit another cigarette. The conversation with Johnny had made him nervous. Why had he said, ‘Some combination of pride and terror’? Did he still think it was uncool to admit to any enthusiasm, even in front of his greatest friend? Why did he muzzle new feelings with old habits of speech? It might not have been obvious to anyone else, but he longed to stop thinking about himself, to stop strip-mining his memories, to stop the introspective and retrospective drift of his thoughts. He wanted to break into a wider world, to learn something, to make a difference.

Above all, he wanted to stop being a child without using the cheap disguise of becoming a parent.

'Not that there's much danger of that,' muttered Patrick, finally getting out of bed and putting on a pair of trousers. The days when he was drawn to the sort of girl who whispered, 'Be careful, I'm not wearing any contraception,' as you came inside her, were almost completely over. He could remember one of them speaking warmly of abortion clinics. 'It's quite luxurious while you're there. A comfortable bed, good food, and you can tell all your secrets to the other girls because you know you're not going to meet them again. Even the operation is rather exciting. It's only afterwards that you get really depressed.'

Patrick ground his cigarette into the ashtray and walked through to the kitchen.

And why did he have to attack Johnny's meetings? They were simply places to confess. Why did he have to make everything so harsh and difficult? On the other hand, what was the point of going somewhere to confess if you weren't going to say the one thing that mattered? There were things he'd never told anyone and never would.

2

Nicholas Pratt, still wearing his pyjamas, waddled back to the bedroom of his house in Clabon Mews, squeezing the letters he had just collected from the doormat and scrutinizing the handwriting on the envelopes to see how many 'serious' invitations they might contain. At sixty-seven his body was as 'well preserved' as his memoirs were 'long awaited'. He had met 'everybody', and had a 'fund of marvellous stories', but discretion had placed its gallant finger on his half-opened lips and he had never started the book which he was widely known to be working on. It was not unusual in what he called the 'big world', namely among the two or three thousand rich people who recognized his name, to hear anxious men and women 'dreading to think' how they had turned out in 'Nicholas's book'.

Collapsing on his bed, where he nowadays slept alone, he was about to test his theory that he had only received three letters that were really worth opening, when he was interrupted by the ringing of the phone.

'Hello,' he yawned.

'Ni-ko-la?' said a brisk woman's voice, pronouncing the name as if it were French. 'It's Jacqueline d'Alantour.'

'*Quel honneur*,' simpered Nicholas in his appalling French accent.

'How are you, darling? I r-ring because Jacques and I are staying at Cheet-lai for Sonny's birthday, and I thought you might be going there too.'

'Of course I am,' said Nicholas sternly. 'In fact, as the patron saint of Bridget's social triumph, I'm meant to be there already. It was I, after all, who introduced little Miss Watson-Scott, as she was then, into the beau monde, as *it* was then, and she has not forgotten her debt to Uncle Nicholas.'

'R-remind me,' said Jacqueline, 'was she one of the ladies you married?'

'Don't be absurd,' said Nicholas, pretending to take offence. 'Just because I've had six failed marriages, there's no need to invent more.'

'But Ni-ko-la, seriously, I r-ring in case you want

to come with us in the car. We have a driver from the embassy. It will be more fun – no? – to go down together, or up together – this English "up" and "down" *c'est vraiment* too much.'

Nicholas was enough of a man of the world to know that the French ambassador's wife was not being entirely altruistic. She was offering him a lift so as to arrive at Cheatley with an intimate friend of Bridget's. Nicholas, for his part, would bring fresh glamour to that intimacy by arriving with the Alantours. They would enhance each other's glory.

'Up or down,' said Nicholas, 'I'd adore to come with you.'

Sonny Gravesend sat in the library at Cheatley dialling the familiar digits of Peter Porlock's number on his radio telephone. The mystical equation between property and person which had so long propped up Sonny's dim personality was worshipped nowhere more ardently than at Cheatley. Peter, George Watford's eldest son, was Sonny's best friend and the only person he really trusted when he wanted sound advice about farming or sex. Sonny sat back in his chair and waited for Peter to wade through the vast rooms of Richfield to the nearest telephone. He looked at the fireplace, above which hung the painting that Robin Parker was taking so long to authenticate as a Poussin. It had been a Poussin when the fourth Earl bought it and, as far as Sonny was concerned, it still was. Nevertheless, one had to get an 'expert opinion'.

'Sonny?' bawled Peter.

'Peter!' Sonny shouted back. 'Sorry to interrupt you again.'

'Quite the opposite, old boy, you've saved me from showing round the Gay London Bikers my old housemaster sent down to gawp at the ceilings.'

'Slaving away as usual,' said Sonny. 'Makes it all the more annoying when one reads the sort of rubbish they put in the papers this morning: "ten thousand acres . . . five hundred guests . . . Princess Margaret . . . party of the year." Sounds as if we're *made* of money, whereas the reality, as nobody knows better than you, with your Gay London Bikers, is that we never stop slaving to keep the rain out.'

'Do you know what one of my tenants said to me the other day after my famous appearance on the box?' Peter adopted his standard yokel accent. '"Saw you on the television, m'lord, pleading poverty, as usual." Damned cheek!'

'It's quite funny, actually.'

'Well, he's really a splendid fellow,' said Peter. 'His family have been tenants of ours for three hundred years.'

'We've got some like that. One lot have been with us for twenty generations.'

'Shows an amazing lack of initiative when you think of the conditions we keep them in,' said Peter mischievously.

Both men guffawed, and agreed that that was just the sort of thing one shouldn't say during one's famous television appearances.

'What I really rang about,' said Sonny, more seriously, 'is this business with Cindy. Bridget, of course, wouldn't have her, on the grounds that we didn't know her, but I've spoken to David Windfall this morning and, since his wife's ill, he's agreed to bring Cindy along. I hope he'll be discreet.'

'David Windfall? You must be joking!' said Peter.

'Well, I know, but I made out that I was longing to meet her, rather than the truth, namely that all my Historic Houses Association and Preservation of Rural England meetings have been one long thrash in the sack with Cindy.'

'I'm glad you didn't tell him that,' said Peter wisely.

'The thing is, and I need hardly tell you to keep this under your hat, the thing is, Cindy's pregnant.'

'Are you sure it's yours?'

'Apparently there's no doubt about it,' said Sonny.

'I suppose she's blackmailing you,' said Peter loyally.

'No, no, no, that's not it at all,' said Sonny, rather put out. 'The thing is, I haven't had "conjugal relations" with Bridget for some time, and I'm not sure anyway, given her age, that it would be a good idea to try and have another child. But, as you know, I'm very keen to have a son, and I thought that if Cindy has a boy . . .' Sonny trailed off, uncertain of Peter's reaction.

'Golly,' said Peter, 'but you'd have to marry her if he was going to inherit. It's one of the penalties of being a peer,' he added with a note of noble stoicism.

'Well, I know it sounds awfully mercenary to chuck Bridget at this stage of the game,' Sonny admitted, 'and of course it's bound to be misrepresented as a sexual infatuation, but one does feel some responsibility towards Cheatley.'

'But think of the expense,' said Peter, who had grave doubts that the divorce could be achieved in time. 'And, besides, is Cindy the right girl for Cheaters?'

'She'll be a breath of fresh air,' said Sonny breezily, 'and, as you know, all the things are in trust.'

'I think,' said Peter with the measured authority of a consultant advising his patient to have surgery, 'we'd better have lunch in Buck's next week.'

'Good idea,' said Sonny. 'See you tonight.'

'Very much looking forward to it,' said Peter. 'Oh, and, by the way, happy birthday.'

Kitty Harrow, at home in the country, lay in bed propped up by a multitude of pillows, her King Charles spaniels hidden in the troughs of her undulating bedspread, and a ravaged breakfast tray abandoned beside her like an exhausted lover. Under a pink satin lampshade, bottles of contradictory medicines crowded the inlaid surface of her bedside table. Her hand rested on the telephone she used ceaselessly every morning between eleven o'clock and lunchtime, or, as on this occasion, until the hairdresser arrived at twelve thirty to rebuild those cliffs of grey hair against which so many upstarts had dashed themselves in vain. When she had found Robin Parker's name in the large red leather address book that was spread open on her lap, she dialled his number and waited impatiently.

'Hello,' said a rather peevish voice.

'Robin, my darling,' warbled Kitty, 'why aren't you here already? Bridget has unloaded some perfectly ghastly people on me, and you, my only ally, are still in London.'

'I had to go to a drinks party last night,' simpered Robin.

'A party in London on a Friday night!' protested Kitty. 'It's the most antisocial thing I've ever heard. I do think people are inconsiderate, not to say cruel. I practically never go to London these days,' she added with a real note of pathos, 'and so I rely terribly on my weekends.'

'Well, I'm coming to the rescue,' said Robin. 'I ought to be leaving for Paddington in five minutes.'

'Thank God,' she continued, 'you'll be here to protect me. I had an obscene telephone call last night.'

'Not again,' sighed Robin.

'He made the most perfectly revolting suggestions,' confided Kitty. 'And so before putting the phone down I said to him, "Young man, I should have to see your face before I allowed you to do any of those things!" He seemed to think I was encouraging him, and rang back the very next minute. I insist on answering the phone myself in the evenings: it's not fair on the servants.'

'It's not fair on you either,' Robin warned her.

'I've been haunted,' growled Kitty, 'by what you told me about those cocks the prudish Popes snapped off the classical statues and stored in the Vatican cellars. I'm not sure *that* wasn't an obscene phone call.'

'That was history of art,' giggled Robin.

'You know how fascinated I am by people's families,' said Kitty. 'Well, now, whenever I think about them, and the dark secrets they all have lurking under the surface, I can't help picturing those crates hidden in the Vatican cellars. You've corrupted my imagination,' she declared. 'Did you know what a dreadful effect you have on people?'

'My conversation will be completely chaste this evening,' threatened Robin. 'But I really ought to be going to the station now.'

'Goodbye,' cooed Kitty, but her need to talk was so imperious that she added conspiratorially, 'Do you know what George Watford told me last night? – he at least was a familiar face. He said that three-quarters of the people in his address book are dead. I told him not to be so morbid. Anyway, what could be more natural at his age: he's well into his eighties.'

'My dear, I'm going to miss my train,' said Robin.

'I used to suffer terribly from train fever,' said Kitty considerately, 'until my wonderful doctor gave me a magic pill, and now I just float on board.'

'Well, I'm going to have to sprint on board,' squealed Robin.

'Goodbye, my dear,' said Kitty, 'I won't delay you a moment longer. Hurry, hurry, hurry.'

Laura Broghlie felt her existence threatened by solitude. Her mind became 'literally blank', as she had told Patrick Melrose during their week-long affair. Five minutes alone, or off the telephone, unless it was spent in the company of a mirror and a great deal of make-up, was more literal blankness than she could stand.

It had taken her ages to get over Patrick's defection. It was not that she had liked him particularly – it never occurred to her to like people while she was using them, and when she had finished using them, it would clearly have been absurd to start liking them – but it was such a *bore* getting a new lover. Being married put some people off, until she made it clear that it was no impediment from her point of view. Laura was married to Angus Broghlie, who was entitled by ancient Scottish custom to call himself 'The Broghlie'. Laura, by the same token, could call herself 'Madame Broghlie', a right she seldom exercised.

Eventually, after a whole fortnight without a lover, she had managed to seduce Johnny Hall, Patrick's best friend. Johnny wasn't as good as Patrick because he worked during the day. Still, as a journalist he could often 'work on a story at home', which was when they could spend the whole day in bed.

Some subtle questioning had established that Johnny didn't yet know about her affair with Patrick, and she had sworn Johnny to secrecy about their own affair. She didn't know whether to be insulted by Patrick's silence or not, but she intended to let Patrick know about Johnny whenever it would cause maximum confusion. She knew that Patrick still found her sexy, even if he had reservations about her personality. Even she had reservations about her personality.

When the phone rang, Laura raised her head and wriggled across the bed.

'Don't answer it,' moaned Johnny, but he knew he

was in a weak position, having left the room earlier to talk to Patrick. He lit a cigarette.

Laura turned to him and stuck her tongue out, hooking her hair behind her ear as she picked up the phone. 'Hello,' she said, suddenly serious.

'Hi.'

'China! God, your party was *so* great,' gasped Laura, pinching her nose with her thumb and index finger and raising her eyes to the ceiling. She had already analysed with Johnny what a failure it had been.

'Did you really think it was a success?' China asked sceptically.

'Of course it was, darling, everybody loved it,' said Laura, grinning at Johnny.

'But everybody got stuck in the downstairs room,' China whined. 'I really hated it.'

'One always hates one's own parties,' said Laura sympathetically, rolling onto her back and stifling a yawn.

'But you really did like it,' pleaded China. 'Promise.'

'Promise,' said Laura, crossing her fingers, her legs, and finally her eyes. Suddenly convulsed with silent giggles, she raised her feet in the air and rocked on the bed.

Johnny watched, amazed by her childishness, faintly contemptuous of the mocking conspiracy into which he was being drawn, but charmed by the contortions of her naked body. He sank back against the pillows, scanning the details which might explain, but only confirmed the mystery of his obsession: the small dark mole on the inner slope of her hip bone, the surprisingly thick golden hair on her forearm, the high arch of her pale feet.

'Is Angus with you?' sighed China.

'No, he's going straight from Scotland to the party. I have to collect him in Cheltenham. It's such a bore, I don't see why he can't get a taxi.'

'Save, save, save,' said China.

'He looked so good on paper,' said Laura, 'but when it comes down to it, he's completely obsessed with whether a cheap-day return is refundable if you don't use the second half, and other fascinating problems of that kind. It makes one long for an extravagant lover.' She allowed one of her knees to flop sideways on the bed.

Johnny took a long drag on his cigarette and smiled at her.

China hesitated and then, spurred on by the thought that Laura's praise of her party might not have been entirely sincere, she said, 'You know there's a rumour going around that you're having an affair with Patrick Melrose.'

'Patrick Melrose,' said Laura, as if she were repeating the name of a fatal disease, 'you must be joking.' She raised her eyebrows at Johnny and putting her hand over the mouthpiece whispered, 'Apparently I'm having an affair with Patrick.'

He flicked up one of his eyebrows and stubbed out his cigarette.

'Who on earth told you that?' she asked China.

'I shouldn't really tell you, but it was Alexander Politsky.'

'Him, I don't even know him.'

'Well, he thinks he knows about you.'

'How pathetic,' said Laura. 'He just wants to get in with you by pretending he knows all about your friends.' Johnny knelt in front of Laura and, catching both her feet, eased her legs apart.

'He said he found out from Ali Montague,' China insisted.

Laura drew in her breath sharply. 'Well, that just proves it's a lie,' she sighed. 'Anyway, I don't even fancy Patrick Melrose,' she added, digging her nails into Johnny's arms.

'Oh, well, you know better than me whether you're having an affair with him or not,' China concluded. 'I'm glad you're not, because personally I find him really tricky . . .'

Laura held the phone in the air so Johnny could hear. 'And,' continued China, 'I can't stand the way he treated Debbie.'

Laura put the phone back to her ear. 'It was disgusting, wasn't it?' she said, grinning at Johnny, who leaned down to bite her neck. 'But who are you going to the party with?' she asked, knowing that China was going alone.

'I'm not going with anybody, but there's someone called Morgan Ballantine,' China put on an unconvincing American accent to pronounce his name, 'who is going to be there, and I'm quite keen on him. He's supposed to have just inherited two hundred and forty million dollars and an amazing gun collection,' she added casually, 'but that's not really the point, I mean, he's *really* sweet.'

'He may be worth two hundred and forty million dollars, but is he going to spend it?' asked Laura, who had bitter experience of how misleading these figures could be. 'That's the real question,' she said, propping herself up on one elbow and effortlessly ignoring the caresses she had found so breathtaking moments before. Johnny stopped and leaned over, partly from curiosity, but also to disguise the fact that his sexual efforts could not compete with the mention of such a large sum of money.

'He did say something rather sinister the other day,' China admitted.

'What?' asked Laura eagerly.

'Well, he said, "I'm too rich to lend money." A friend of his had gone bankrupt, or something.'

'Don't touch him,' said Laura, in her special serious voice. 'That's the kind of thing Angus says. You think it's all going to be private planes, and the next thing you know he's asking for a doggy bag in a restaurant, or implying that *you* ought to be doing the cooking. It's a complete nightmare.'

'That reminds me,' said China, rather annoyed that she had given so much away. 'We played a wonderful game after you left last night. Everybody had to think of the things people were least likely to say, and someone came up with one for Angus: "Are you sure you won't have the lobster?"'

'Very funny,' said Laura drily.

'By the way, where are you staying?' asked China.

'With some people called Bossington-Lane.'

'Me too,' exclaimed China. 'Can I have a lift?'

'Of course. Come here about twelve thirty and we can go out to lunch.'

'Perfect,' said China. 'See you later.'

'Bye, darling,' Laura trilled. 'Stupid cow,' she said, putting the phone down.

All her life men had rushed around Cindy, like the citizens of Lilliput with their balls of string, trying to tie her down so she wouldn't wreck their little lives, but now she was thinking of tying herself down voluntarily.

'Hello?' she purred in her soft Californian accent. 'Can I speak with David Windfall, please?'

'Speaking,' said David.

'Hi there, I'm Cindy Smith. I guess Sonny already talked to you about tonight.'

'He certainly did,' said David, flushing to a deeper shade of raspberry than usual.

'I hope you've got your Sonny and Bridget invitation, 'cause I sure don't have one,' said Cindy with disarming candour.

'I've got mine in the bank,' said David. 'One can't be too careful.'

'I know,' said Cindy, 'that's a valuable item.'

'You realize you'll have to pretend to be my wife,' said David.

'How far am I meant to go?'

David, quivering, sweating, and blushing at the same time, took refuge in the bluffness for which he was well known. 'Only until we get past the security people,' he said.

'Anything you say,' Cindy replied meekly. 'You're the boss.'

'Where shall we meet?' asked David.

'I've got a suite in the Little Soddington House Hotel. That's in Gloucestershire, right?'

'I certainly hope so, unless it's moved,' said David, more pompously than he'd intended.

Cindy giggled. 'Sonny didn't tell me you were so funny,' she said. 'We could have dinner together at my hotel, if you'd like.'

'Splendid,' said David, already scheming to get out of the dinner party Bridget had put him in. 'About eight?'

*

Tom Charles had ordered a car to take him down to the country. It was extravagant, but he was too old to fool around with trains and suitcases. He was staying at Claridge's, as usual, and one of the nicest things about it was the wood fire that was subsiding brightly in the grate while he finished his frugal breakfast of tea and grapefruit juice.

He was on his way to stay with Harold Greene, an old friend from the IMF days. Harold had said to bring a dinner jacket because they were going to a neighbour's birthday party. He'd got the low-down on the neighbour, but all Tom could remember was that he was one of those Englishmen with plenty of 'background' and not a hell of a lot going on in the foreground. If you weren't unduly impressed by these 'background' types they said you were 'chippy', but in fact nothing could make you feel less 'chippy' than contemplating a lifetime wasted in gossip, booze, and sexual intrigue.

Harold was not like that at all; he was a mover and shaker. He was on the Christmas-card list of grateful presidents and friendly senators – as was Tom – but like everybody else on this rainy island he liked the 'background' types too much.

Tom picked up the phone to ring Anne Eisen.

Anne was an old friend and he was looking forward to driving down with her to Harold's, but he had to know what time to send the car to collect her. Her number was engaged and so Tom hung up crisply and continued reading the pile of English and American newspapers he'd ordered with his breakfast.

3

Tony Fowles was what Bridget called an 'absolute genius' when it came to colours and fabrics. He confessed to 'having a crush on ash colours at the moment,' and she had agreed to have the interior of the tent done in grey. Her initial misgivings about this bold idea were swept aside by Tony's remark that Jacqueline d'Alantour, the French Ambassador's wife, was 'so correct that she's never really *right*'.

Bridget wondered how far one could be incorrect without being wrong, and it was in this grey area that Tony had become her guide, increasing her dependency on him until she could hardly light a cigarette without his assistance, and had already had a row with Sonny about wanting to have him at her side during dinner.

'That appalling little man shouldn't be coming at

all,' said Sonny, 'let alone sitting next to you. I need hardly remind you that we're having Princess Margaret for dinner and that every one of the men has a better claim to be by your side than that . . .' Sonny spluttered, 'that popinjay.'

What was a popinjay anyway? Whatever it was, it was so unfair, because Tony was her guru and her jester. People who knew how funny he was – and one only had to hear his story about hurrying through the streets of Lima clutching bolts of fabric during a bread riot to practically die laughing – didn't perhaps realize how wise he was also.

But where was Tony? He was supposed to meet her at eleven o'clock. One could worship him for all sorts of things, but punctuality wasn't one of them. Bridget looked around at the wastes of grey velvet that lined the inside of the tent; without Tony, her confidence faltered. One end of the tent was dominated by a hideous white stage on which a forty-piece band, flown over from America, would later play the 'traditional New Orleans jazz' favoured by Sonny. The industrial heaters that roared in every corner still left the atmosphere numbingly cold.

'Obviously, I'd rather that my birthday was in June

instead of gloomy old February,' Sonny was fond of saying, 'but one can't choose when one's born.'

The shock of not having planned his own birth had given Sonny a fanatical desire to plan everything else. Bridget had tried to keep him out of the tent on the grounds that it should be a 'surprise', but since this word was for him roughly equivalent to 'terrorist outrage', she had failed. She had, on the other hand, managed to keep secret the astonishing cost of the velvet, communicated to her by a honking Sloane with a laugh like a death rattle, who had said that it came to 'forty thousand, plus the dreaded'. Bridget had thought 'the dreaded' was a technical decorating term until Tony explained that it was VAT.

He had also said that the orange lilies would make a 'riot of colour' against the soft grey background, but now that they were being arranged by a team of busy ladies in chequered blue overalls, Bridget could not help thinking they looked more like dying embers in a huge heap of ash.

Just as this heretical thought was entering her mind, Tony swept into the tent dressed in a baggy earth, ash, and grape sweater, a pair of beautifully ironed jeans, white socks, and brown moccasins with surprisingly thick soles. He had wrapped a white silk scarf around his throat after he felt, or thought he felt, a tickle. 'Tony! At last,' Bridget dared to point out.

'I'm sorry,' croaked Tony, laying his hand on his chest and frowning pathetically. 'I think I'm coming down with something.'

'Oh, dear,' said Bridget, 'I hope you won't be too ill for tonight.'

'Even if they had to wheel me in on a life-support machine,' he replied, 'I wouldn't miss it for the world. I know the artist is supposed to stand outside his creation, paring his fingernails,' he said, looking down at his fingernails with affected indifference, 'but I don't feel my creation is finished until it's filled with living fabric.'

He paused and stared at Bridget with hypnotic intensity, like Rasputin about to inform the Tsarina of his latest inspiration. 'Now, I know what you're thinking,' he assured her. 'Not enough colour!'

Bridget felt a searchlight shining into the recesses of her soul. 'The flowers haven't changed it as much as I thought they would,' she confessed.

'And that's why I've brought you these,' said Tony, pointing to a group of assistants who had been waiting meekly until they were called forward. They were surrounded by large cardboard boxes.

'What are they?' asked Bridget, apprehensive.

The assistants started to open the tops of the boxes. 'I thought tents, I thought poles, I thought ribbons,' said Tony, who was always ready to explain his imaginative processes. 'And so I had these specially made. It's a sort of regimental-maypole theme,' he explained, no longer able to contain his excitement. 'It'll look stunning against the pearly texture of the ash.'

Bridget knew that 'specially made' meant extremely expensive. 'They look like ties,' she said, peering into a box.

'Exactly,' said Tony triumphantly. 'I saw Sonny wearing a rather thrilling green and orange tie. He told me it was a regimental tie and I thought, that's it: the orange will pick up the lilies and lift the whole room.' Tony's hands flowed upward and outward. 'We'll tie the ribbons to the top of the pole and bring them over to the sides of the tent.' This time his hands flowed outwards and downward.

These graceful balletic gestures were enough to convince Bridget that she had no choice.

'It sounds wonderful,' she said. 'But put them up quickly, we haven't much time.'

'Leave it to me,' said Tony serenely.

A maid came to tell Bridget that there was a phone call for her. Bridget waved goodbye to Tony, and hurried out of the tent through the red-carpeted tunnel that led back to the house. Smiling florists arranged wreaths of ivy around the green metal hoops that supported the canvas.

It was strange, in February, not to give the party in the house, but Sonny was convinced that his 'things' would be imperilled by what he called 'Bridget's London friends'. He was haunted by his grandfather's complaint that his grandmother had filled the house with 'spongers, buggers, and Jews', and, while he recognized the impossibility of giving an amusing party without samples from all these categories, he wasn't about to trust them with his 'things'.

Bridget walked across the denuded drawing room, and picked up the phone.

'Hello?'

'Darling, how are you?'

'Aurora! Thank God it's you. I was dreading another virtual stranger begging to bring their entire family to the party.'

'Aren't people *awful*?' said Aurora Donne in that condescending voice for which she was famous. Her large liquid eyes and creamy complexion gave her the soft beauty of a Charolais cow, but her sniggering laughter, reserved for her own remarks, was more reminiscent of a hyena. She had become Bridget's best friend, instilling her with a grim and precarious confidence in exchange for Bridget's lavish hospitality.

'It's been a nightmare,' said Bridget, settling down in the spindly caterer's chair that had replaced one of Sonny's things. 'I can't believe the cheek of some of these people.'

'You don't have to tell me,' said Aurora. 'I hope you've got good security.'

'Yes,' said Bridget. 'Sonny's got the police, who were supposed to be at a football match this afternoon, to come here instead and check everything. It makes a nice change for them. They're going to form a ring around the house. Plus, we've got the usual people at the door, in fact, someone called "Gresham Security" has left his walkie-talkie by the phone.'

'They make such a fuss about royalty,' said Aurora.

'*Don't*,' groaned Bridget. 'We've had to give up two of our precious rooms to the private detective and the lady-in-waiting. It's such a waste of space.'

Bridget was interrupted by the sound of screaming in the hall.

'You're a filthy little girl! And nothing but a burden to your parents!' shouted a woman with a strong Scottish accent. 'What would the Princess say if she knew that you dirtied your dress? You filthy child!'

'Oh dear,' said Bridget to Aurora, 'I do wish Nanny wasn't quite so horrid to Belinda. It's rather terrible, but I never dare say anything to her.'

'I know,' said Aurora sympathetically, 'I'm absolutely terrified of Lucy's nanny. I think it's because she reminds one of one's own nanny.'

Bridget, who had not had a 'proper' nanny, wasn't about to reveal this fact by disagreeing. She had made a special effort, by way of compensation, to get a proper old-fashioned nanny for seven-year-old Belinda. The agency had been delighted when they found such a good position for the vicious old bag who'd been on their books for years.

'The other thing I dread is my mother coming tonight,' said Bridget.

'Mothers can be so critical, can't they?' said Aurora.

'Exactly,' said Bridget, who in fact found her mother tiresomely eager to please. 'I suppose I ought to go off and be nice to Belinda,' she added with a dutiful sigh.

'Sweet!' cooed Aurora.

'I'll see you tonight, darling.' Bridget was grateful

to get rid of Aurora. She had a million and one things to do and besides, instead of giving her those transfusions of self-confidence for which she was, well, almost employed (she didn't have a bean), Aurora had recently taken to implying that she would have handled the arrangements for the party better than Bridget.

Given that she had no intention of going up to see Belinda it was quite naughty to have used her as an excuse to end the conversation. Bridget seldom found the time to see her daughter. She could not forgive her for being a girl and burdening Sonny with the anxiety of having no heir. After spending her early twenties having abortions, Bridget had spent the next ten years having miscarriages. Successfully giving birth had been complicated enough without having a child of the wrong gender. The doctor had told her that it would be dangerous to try again, and at forty-two she was becoming resigned to having one child, especially in view of Sonny's reluctance to go to bed with her.

Her looks had certainly deteriorated over the last sixteen years of marriage. The clear blue eyes had clouded over, the candlelit glow of her skin had sputtered out and could only be partially rekindled with tinted creams, and the lines of her body, which had shaped so many obsessions in their time, were now deformed by accumulations of stubborn fat. Unwilling to betray Sonny, and unable to attract him, Bridget had allowed herself to go into a mawkish physical decline, spending more and more time thinking of other ways to please her husband – or rather not to displease him, since he took her efforts for granted but lavished his attention on the slightest failure.

She ought to get on with the arrangements, which, in her case, meant worrying, since all the work had been delegated to somebody else. The first thing she decided to worry about was the walkie-talkie on the table beside her. It had clearly been lost by some hopeless security man. Bridget picked the machine up and, curious, switched it on. There was a loud hissing sound and then the whinings of an untuned radio.

Interested to see if she could make anything intelligible emerge from this melee of sound, Bridget got up and walked around the room. The noises grew louder and fainter, and sometimes intensified into squeals, but as she moved towards the windows, darkened by the side of the marquee that reared up wet and white under the dull winter sky, she heard, or thought she heard, a voice. Pressing her ear close to the walkie-talkie she could make out a crackling, whispering conversation.

'The thing is, I haven't had conjugal relations with Bridget for some time . . .' said the voice at the other end, and faded again. Bridget shook the walkie-talkie desperately, and moved closer to the window. She couldn't understand what was going on. How could it be Sonny she was listening to? But who else could claim that he hadn't had 'conjugal relations' with her for some time?

She could make out words again, and pressed the walkie-talkie to her ear with renewed curiosity and dread.

'To chuck Bridget at this . . . it's bound to be . . . but one does feel some responsibility towards . . .' Interference drowned the conversation again. A prickling wave of heat rushed over her body. She must hear what they were saying, what monstrous plan they were hatching. Who was Sonny talking to? It must be Peter. But what if it wasn't? What if he talked like this to everyone, everyone except her?

'All the things are in trust,' she heard, and then another voice saying: 'Lunch . . . next week.' Yes, it was Peter. There was more crackling, and then, 'Happy birthday.'

Bridget sank down in the window seat. She raised her arm and almost flung the walkie-talkie against the wall, but then lowered it again slowly until it hung loosely by her side.

4

Johnny Hall had been going to Narcotics Anonymous meetings for over a year. In a fit of enthusiasm and humility he found hard to explain, he had volunteered to make the tea and coffee at the Saturday three o'clock meeting. He recognized many of the people who took one of the white plastic cups he had filled with a tea bag or a few granules of instant coffee, and struggled to remember their names, embarrassed that so many of them remembered his.

After making the tea Johnny took a seat in the back row, as usual, although he knew that it would make it harder for him to speak, or 'share', as he was urged to say in meetings. He enjoyed the obscurity of sitting as far away as possible from the addict who was 'giving the chair'. The 'preamble' – a ritual reading of selections from 'the literature', explaining the nature of addiction and NA – washed over Johnny almost unnoticed. He tried to see if the girl sitting in the front row was pretty, but couldn't see enough of her profile to judge.

A woman called Angie had been asked by the secretary to do the chair. Her stumpy legs were clad in a black leotard, and her hair hid two-thirds of her raddled and exhausted face. She had been invited down from Kilburn to add a touch of grit to a Chelsea meeting which dwelt all too often on the shame of burgling one's parents' house, or the difficulty of finding a parking space.

Angie said she had started 'using', by which she meant taking drugs, in the sixties, because it was 'a gas'. She didn't want to dwell on the 'bad old days', but she had to tell the group a little bit about her using to put them in the picture. Half an hour later, she was still describing her wild twenties, and yet there was clearly some time to go before her listeners could enjoy the insight that she had gleaned from her regular attendance of meetings over the last two years. She rounded off her chair with some self-deprecating remarks about still being 'riddled with defects'. Thanks to the meetings she had discovered that she was totally insane and completely addicted to everything. She was also 'rampantly co-dependent', and urgently needed individual counselling in order to deal with lots of 'childhood stuff'. Her 'relationship', by which she meant her boyfriend, had discovered that living with an addict could create a lot of extra hassles, and so the two of them had decided to attend 'couples counselling'. This was the latest excitement in a life already packed with therapeutic drama, and she was very hopeful about the benefits.

The secretary was very grateful to Angie. A lot of what she had shared, he said, was relevant for him too. He'd 'identified one hundred per cent', not with her using because his had been very different – he had never used needles or been addicted to heroin or cocaine – but with 'the feelings'. Johnny could not remember Angie describing any feelings, but tried to silence the scepticism which made it so difficult for him to participate in the meetings, even after the breakthrough of volunteering to make the tea. The secretary went on to say that a lot of childhood stuff had been coming up for him too, and he had recently discovered that although nothing unpleasant had happened to him in childhood, he'd found himself smothered by his parents' kindness and that breaking away from their understanding and generosity had become a real issue for him.

With these resonant words the secretary threw the meeting open, a moment that Johnny always found upsetting because it put him under pressure to 'share'. The problem, apart from his acute self-consciousness and his resistance to the language of 'recovery', was that sharing was supposed to be based on 'identification' with something that the person who was doing the chair had said, and it was very rare for Johnny to have any clear recollection of what had been said. He decided to wait until somebody else's identification identified for him the details of Angie's chair. This was a hazardous procedure because most of the time people identified with something that had not in fact been said in the chair.

The first person to speak from the floor said that he'd had to nurture himself by 'parenting the child within'. He hoped that with God's help – a reference that always made Johnny wince – and the help of the Fellowship, the child within would grow up in a 'safe environment'. He said that he too was having problems with his relationship, by which he meant his girlfriend, but that hopefully, if he worked his Step Three and 'handed it over', everything would be all right in the end. He wasn't in charge of the results, only the 'footwork'.

The second speaker identified one hundred per cent with what Angie had said about her veins being 'the envy of Kilburn', because his veins had been the envy of Wimbledon. There was general merriment. And yet, the speaker went on to say, when he had to go to the doctor nowadays for a proper medical reason, they couldn't find a vein anywhere on his body. He had been doing a Step Four, 'a fearless and searching moral inventory', and it had brought up a lot of stuff that needed looking at. He had heard someone in a meeting saying that she had a fear of success and he thought that maybe this was his problem too. He was in a lot of pain at the moment because he was realizing that a lot of his 'relationship problems' were the result of his 'dysfunctional family'. He felt unlovable and consequently he was unloving, he concluded, and his neighbour, who recognized that he was in the presence of feelings, rubbed his back consolingly.

Johnny looked up at the fluorescent lights and the white polystyrene ceiling of the dingy church-hall basement. He longed to hear someone talk about their experiences in ordinary language, and not in this obscure and fatuous slang. He was entering the stage of the meeting when he gave up daydreaming and became increasingly anxious about whether to speak. He constructed opening sentences, imagined elegant ways of linking what had been said to what he wanted to say, and then, with a thumping heart, failed to announce his name quickly enough to win the right to speak. He was particularly restless after the show of coolness he always felt he had to put on in front of Patrick. Talking to Patrick had exacerbated his rebellion against the foolish vocabulary of NA, while increasing his need for the peace of mind that others seemed to glean from using it. He regretted agreeing to have dinner alone with Patrick, whose corrosive criticism and drug nostalgia and stylized despair often left Johnny feeling agitated and confused.

The current speaker was saying that he'd read somewhere in the literature that the difference between 'being willing' and 'being ready' was that you could sit in an armchair and be willing to leave the house, but you weren't entirely ready until you had on your hat and overcoat. Johnny knew that the speaker must be finishing, because he was using Fellowship platitudes, trying to finish on a 'positive' note, as was the custom of the obedient recovering addict, who always claimed to bear in mind 'newcomers' and their need to hear positive notes.

He must do it, he must break in now, and say his piece.

'My name's Johnny,' he blurted out, almost before the previous speaker had finished. 'I'm an addict.'

'Hi, Johnny,' chorused the rest of the group.

'I have to speak,' he said boldly, 'because I'm going to a party this evening, and I know there'll be a lot of drugs around. It's a big party and I just feel under threat, I suppose. I just wanted to come to this meeting to reaffirm my desire to stay clean today. Thanks.'

'Thanks, Johnny,' the group echoed.

He'd done it, he'd said what was really troubling him. He hadn't managed to say anything funny, clever, or interesting, but he knew that somehow, however ridiculous and boring these meetings were, having taken part in one would give him the strength not to take drugs at the party tonight and that he would be able to enjoy himself a little bit more.

Glowing with goodwill after speaking, Johnny listened to Pete, the next speaker, with more sympathy than he'd been able to muster at the beginning of the meeting.

Someone had described recovery to Pete as 'putting your tie around your neck instead of your arm'. There was subdued laughter. When he was using, Pete had found it easy to cross the road because he didn't care whether he was run over or not, but in early recovery he'd become fucking terrified of the traffic (subdued laughter) and walked for miles and miles to find a zebra crossing. He'd also spent his early recovery making lines out of Colman's mustard powder and wondering if he'd put too much in the spoon (one isolated cackle). He was 'in bits' at the moment because he had broken up with his relationship. She'd wanted him to be some kind of trout fisherman, and he'd wanted her to be a psychiatric nurse. When she'd left she'd said that she still thought he was the 'best thing on two legs'. It had worried him that she'd fallen in love with a pig (laughter). Or a centipede (more laughter). Talk about pushing his shame buttons! He'd been on a 'Step Twelve Call' the other day, by which he meant a visit to an active addict who had rung the NA office, and the guy was in a dreadful state, but frankly, Pete admitted, he had wanted what the other guy had more than the other guy wanted what he had. That was the insanity of the disease! 'I came to this programme on my knees,' concluded

Pete in a more pious tone, 'and it's been suggested that I remain on them' (knowing grunts, and an appreciative, 'Thanks, Pete').

The American girl who spoke after Pete was called Sally. 'Sleeping at night and staying awake during the day' had been 'a real concept' for her when she 'first came round'. What she wanted from the programme was 'wall-to-wall freedom', and she knew she could achieve that with the help of a 'Loving Higher Power'. At Christmas she'd been to a pantomime to 'celebrate her inner child'. Since then she'd been travelling with another member of the Fellowship because, like they said in the States, 'When you're sick together, you stick together.'

After the group had thanked Sally, the secretary said that they were in 'Newcomer's Time' and that he would appreciate it if people would respect that. This announcement was almost always followed by a brief silence for the Newcomer who either didn't exist, or was too terrified to speak. The last five minutes would then be hogged by some old hand who was 'in bits' or 'just wanted to feel part of the meeting'. On this occasion, however, there was a genuine Newcomer in the room, and he dared to open his mouth.

Dave, as he was called, was at his first meeting and

he didn't see how it was supposed to stop him taking drugs. He'd been about to go, actually, and then someone had said about the mustard and the spoon and making lines, and like he'd thought he was the only person to have ever done that, and it was funny hearing someone else say it. He didn't have any money, and he couldn't go out because he owed money everywhere: the only reason he wasn't stoned was that he didn't have the energy to steal anymore. He still had his TV, but he had this thing that he was controlling it, and he was afraid of watching it now because last night he'd been worried that he'd been putting the bloke on TV off by staring at him. He couldn't think what else to say.

The secretary thanked him in the especially coaxing voice he used for Newcomers whose distress formed his own spiritual nourishment, an invaluable opportunity to 'give it away' and 'pass on the message'. He advised Dave to stick around after the meeting and get some phone numbers. Dave said his phone had been cut off. The secretary, afraid that magical 'sharing' might degenerate into mere conversation, smiled firmly at Dave and asked if there were any more Newcomers.

Johnny, somewhat to his surprise, found himself

caring about what happened to Dave. In fact, he really hoped that these people, people like him who had been hopelessly dependent on drugs, obsessed with them, and unable to think about anything else for years, would get their lives together. If they had to use this obscure slang in order to do so, then that was a pity but not a reason to hope that they would fail.

The secretary said that unless there was somebody who urgently needed to share, they were out of time. Nobody spoke, and so he stood up and asked Angie to help him close the meeting. Everybody else stood up as well and held hands.

'Will you join me in the Serenity Prayer,' asked Angie, 'using the word "God" as you understand him, her, or it. God,' she said to kickstart the prayer, and then when everyone was ready to join in, repeated, 'God, grant me the serenity to accept the things I cannot change, The courage to change the things I can, And the wisdom to know the difference.'

Johnny wondered as usual to whom he was addressing this prayer. Sometimes when he got chatting to his 'fellow addicts' he would admit to being 'stuck on Step Three'. Step Three made the bold suggestion that he hand his will and his life over to God 'as he understood him'.

At the end of the meeting, Amanda Pratt, whom he hadn't noticed until then, came up to him. Amanda was the twenty-two-year-old daughter of Nicholas Pratt by his most sensible wife, the general's daughter with the blue woolly and the simple string of pearls he used to dream gloomily of marrying when he was going out with Bridget.

Johnny did not know Amanda well, but he somehow knew this story about her parents. She was eight years younger than him, and to Johnny she was not a drug addict at all, just one of those neurotic girls who had taken a bit of coke or speed to help her dieting, and a few sleeping pills to help her sleep, and, worst of all, when these pitiful abuses had started to become unpleasant, she had stopped them. Johnny, who had wasted his entire twenties repeating the same mistakes, took a very condescending view of anybody who came to the end of their tether before him, or for less good reasons.

'It was so funny,' Amanda was saying rather louder than Johnny would have liked, 'when you were sharing about going to a big party tonight, I knew it was Cheatley.'

'Are you going?' asked Johnny, already knowing the answer.

'Oh, ya,' said Amanda. 'Bridget's practically a stepmother, because she went out with Daddy just before he married Mummy.'

Johnny looked at Amanda and marvelled again at the phenomenon of pretty girls who were not at all sexy. Something empty and clinging about her, a missing centre, prevented her from being attractive.

'Well, we'll see each other tonight,' said Johnny, hoping to end the conversation.

'You're a friend of Patrick Melrose, aren't you?' asked Amanda, immune to the finality of his tone.

'Yes,' said Johnny.

'Well, I gather he spends a lot of time slagging off the Fellowship,' said Amanda indignantly.

'Can you blame him?' sighed Johnny, looking over Amanda's shoulder to see if Dave was still in the room.

'Yes, I do blame him,' said Amanda. 'I think it's rather pathetic, actually, and it just shows how sick he is: if he wasn't sick, he wouldn't need to slag off the Fellowship.'

'You're probably right,' said Johnny, resigned to the familiar tautologies of 'recovery'. 'But listen, I have to go now, or I'll miss my lift down to the country.'

'See you tonight,' said Amanda cheerfully. 'I may need you for an emergency meeting!'

'Umm,' said Johnny. 'It's nice to know you'll be there.'

5

Robin Parker was horrified to see, through the pebble spectacles which helped him to distinguish fake Poussins from real ones, but could not, alas, make him a safe driver, that an old woman had moved into 'his' compartment during the ordeal he had just undergone of fetching a miniature gin and tonic from the squalid buffet. Everything about the train offended him: the plastic 'glass', the purple-and-turquoise upholstery, the smell of diesel and dead skin, and now the invasion of his compartment by an unglamorous personage wearing an overcoat that only the Queen could have hoped to get away with. He pursed his lips as he squeezed past an impossible pale-blue nanny's suitcase that the old woman had left cluttering the floor. Picking up his copy of the *Spectator*, a Perseus's shield against the Medusa of modernity, as he'd said more than once, he lapsed into a daydream in which he was flown *privately* into Gloucestershire from Zurich or possibly Deauville, with someone really glamorous. And as he pretended to read, passing through Charlbury and Moreton-in-Marsh, he imagined the clever and subtle things he would have said about the Ben Nicholsons on the wall of the cabin.

Virginia Watson-Scott glanced nervously at her suitcase, knowing it was in everybody's way. The last time she'd been on a train, a kind young man had hoisted it into the luggage rack without sparing a thought for how she was going to get it down again. She'd been too polite to say anything, but she could remember tottering under the weight as the train drew in to Paddington. Even so, the funny-looking gentleman opposite might at least have offered.

In the end she'd decided not to pack the burgundy velvet dress she'd bought for the party. She had lost her nerve, something that would never have happened when Roddy was alive, and fallen back on an old favourite that Sonny and Bridget had seen a hundred times before, or would have seen a hundred times if they asked her to Cheatley more often.

She knew what it was, of course: Bridget was

embarrassed by her. Sonny was somehow gallant and rude at the same time, full of old-fashioned courtesies that failed to disguise his underlying contempt. She didn't care about him, but it did hurt to think that her daughter didn't want her around. Old people were always saying that they didn't want to be a burden. Well, she *did* want to be a burden. It wasn't as if she would be taking the last spare room, just one of Sonny's cottages. He was always boasting about how many he had and what a terrible responsibility they were.

Bridget had been such a nice little girl. It was that horrible Nicholas Pratt who had changed her. It was hard to describe, but she had started to criticize everything at home, and look down her nose at people she'd known all her life. Virginia had only met Nicholas once, thank goodness, when he had taken her and Roddy to the opera. She had said to Roddy afterwards that Nicholas wasn't her cup of tea at all, but Roddy had said that Bridget was a sensible girl and she was old enough now to make her own decisions.

'Oh, do come on,' said Caroline Porlock. 'We promised to arrive early and lend moral support.'

Moral support, thought Peter Porlock, still dazed

from his conversation with Sonny that morning, was certainly what Cheatley needed.

They headed down the drive past placid deer and old oaks. Peter reflected that he was one of those Englishmen who could truly claim that his home was his castle, and wondered whether that was the sort of thing to say during one's famous television appearances. On balance, he decided, as Caroline whizzed the Subaru through the honey-coloured gateposts, probably not.

Nicholas Pratt lounged in the back of the Alantours' car. This is how the world should be seen, he thought: through the glass partition of a limousine.

The rack of lamb had been excellent, the cheeses flown in from France that morning, delicious, and the 1970 Haut Brion, '*très buvable*,' as the ambassador had modestly remarked.

'*Et la comtesse, est-elle bien née?*' asked Jacqueline, returning to the subject of Bridget, so that her husband could savour the details of her background.

'*Pas du tout*,' answered Nicholas in a strong English accent.

'Not quite from the top basket!' exclaimed Jacques

d'Alantour, who prided himself on his command of colloquial English.

Jacqueline was not quite from the top basket herself, reflected Nicholas, which was what gave that rather hungry quality to her fascination with social standing. Her mother had been the daughter of a Lebanese arms dealer, and had married Phillipe du Tant, a penniless and obscure baron who had neither been able to spoil her like her father, nor to save her from being spoilt. Jacqueline had not been born so much as numbered, somewhere in the Union des Banques Suisses. With the slightly sallow complexion and downturned mouth she had inherited from her mother, she could have done without the frighteningly prominent nose that her father had settled on her; but already famous as an heiress from an early age, she appeared to most people as a photograph come to life, a name made flesh, a bank account personified.

'Is that why you didn't marry her?' teased Jacqueline.

'I'm quite *bien né* enough for two,' replied Nicholas grandly. 'But, you know, I'm not the snob I used to be.'

The ambassador raised his finger in judgement. 'You are a better snob!' he declared, with a witty expression on his face.

'There are so many varieties of snobbism,' said Jacqueline, 'one cannot admire all of them.'

'Snobbery is one of the things one should be most discriminating about,' said Nicholas.

'Some things, like not tolerating stupid people, or not having pigs at one's table, are not snobbish at all, they are simply common sense,' said Jacqueline.

'And yet,' said the wily ambassador, 'sometimes it is necessary to have pigs at one's table.'

Diplomats, thought Nicholas, long made redundant by telephones, still preserved the mannerisms of men who were dealing with great matters of state. He had once seen Jacques d'Alantour fold his overcoat on a banister and declare with all the emphasis of a man refusing to compromise over the Spanish Succession, 'I shall put my coat *here*.' He had then placed his hat on a nearby chair and added with an air of infinite subtlety, 'But my hat I shall put *here*. Otherwise it may fall!' as if he were hinting that on the other hand some arrangement could be reached over the exact terms of the marriage.

'If they are at one's table,' concluded Jacqueline tolerantly, 'they are no longer pigs.'

*

Obeying the law that people always loathe those they have wronged, Sonny found himself especially allergic to Bridget after his conversation with Peter Porlock, and went as far as the nursery to avoid her.

'Dada! What are you doing here?' asked Belinda.

'I've come to see my favourite girl,' boomed Sonny.

'What a lucky girl you are,' cooed Nanny, 'a busy man like your father coming to see you on a day like this!'

'That's all right, Nanny,' said Sonny. 'I'll take over.'

'Yes, sir,' said Nanny unctuously.

'Well,' said Sonny, rubbing his hands together, 'what have you been up to?'

'We were reading a book!'

'What's the story about?' asked Sonny.

'It's a school trip,' said Belinda rather shyly.

'And where do they go?'

'To the wax museum.'

'Madame Tussaud's?'

'Yes, and Tim and Jane are very naughty and they stay behind and hide, and when it's night-time all the wax people come to life, and then they start to dance with each other like real people, and they make friends with the children. Will you read it to me, Dada, please?'

'But you've just read it,' said Sonny, puzzled.

'It's my favourite story, and it's better if you read it. *Please*,' pleaded Belinda.

'Of course I will. I'd be delighted,' said Sonny with a little bow, as if he'd been asked to address an agricultural fair. Since he was in the nursery he might as well create a good impression. Besides, he was jolly fond of Belinda and there was no harm in underlining the fact. It was awful to think this way, but one had to be practical and plan ahead and think of Cheatley. Nanny would be a useful character witness if there was a fuss about custody. One could be sure that this unexpected swoop into the nursery would be branded on her memory. Sonny installed himself in an old battered armchair and Belinda, hardly believing her luck, sat in his lap and rested her head against the soft cashmere of his bright red sweater.

'All the children in Tim and Jane's class were very excited,' boomed Sonny. 'They were going on a trip to London . . .'

'It's too bad your not being able to come,' said David Windfall to his wife, slipping a couple of condoms into the inside pocket of his dinner jacket, just in case.

'Have fun, darling,' gasped Jane, longing for him to leave.

'It won't be fun without you,' said David, wondering whether two condoms were enough.

'Don't be silly, darling, you'll forget about me on the motorway.'

David couldn't be bothered to contradict the truth of this assertion.

'I hope you feel better tomorrow,' he said instead. 'I'll call you first thing.'

'You're an angel,' said his wife. 'Drive carefully.'

Johnny had called to say that he would take his own car after all, and so Patrick left London alone, relieved to get away before it was dark. He marvelled at the feverish excitement he had once been able to put into partygoing. It had been based on the hope, never yet fulfilled, that he would stop worrying and stop feeling pointless once the movie of his life took on the appearance of flawless glamour. For this to work, though, he would have had to allow the perspective of a stranger leafing through the filled pages of his diary to eclipse his own point of view, and he would have had to believe, which was far from being the case, that if he got enough reflected glory he could be spared the trouble of seeking out any of his own. Without this snobbish fever he was stranded under the revolving ceiling fan of his own consciousness, taking shallow breaths to get as little oxygen as possible into a brain apparently unable to manufacture anything but dread and regret.

Patrick rewound Iggy Pop's 'The Passenger' for the third time. His car shot down the hill towards the viaduct suspended between the factories and houses of High Wycombe. Released from the trance of the music, a fragment of the dream he'd forgotten that morning came back to him. He could picture an obese Alsatian flinging itself against a padlocked gate, the rattling of the gate. He'd been walking along the path next to a garden, and the dog had been barking at him through the green chicken wire that so often marks the boundary of a French suburban garden.

His car swept up the hill on the other side of the viaduct while the introductory notes of the song strummed through the speakers. Patrick contorted his face, preparing to sing along with Iggy, starting to shout out the familiar words half a beat too early. The smoke-filled car sped tunelessly on into the gathering darkness.

*

One of the reservations Laura had about her personality was that she sometimes got this thing about leaving her flat. She couldn't get through the door, or if she did she had to double back, she just *had* to. Lost and forgotten objects surfaced in her bag the moment she stepped back inside. It had grown worse since her cat died. Making sure the cat had water and food before she went out, and making sure it didn't follow her into the corridor, had helped a lot.

She had just sent China off to fetch the car with the excuse that the bags were too bulky to carry far, but really so that China didn't witness the propitiatory ritual that enabled Laura to get out of the flat. She had to walk out backwards – it was ridiculous, she knew it was ridiculous – and touch the top of the door frame as she went through. There was always the danger of one of her neighbours finding her reversing out of her flat on tiptoe with her arms outstretched, and so she glanced down the corridor first to check that it was clear.

'We could play a game in the car,' China had said. 'The person you'd least like to sit next to at dinner.'

'We've played that before,' Laura had complained.

'But we could play it from other people's point of view.'

'Oh, I hadn't thought of that,' Laura had said.

Anyhow, thought Laura as she locked her front door, Johnny was China's ex-boyfriend and so at least she could have some fun on the drive down, asking about his habits and about how much China missed him.

Alexander Politsky, whose extreme Englishness derived from his being Russian, was perhaps the last man in England to use the term 'old bean' sincerely. He was also widely acknowledged to have the best collection of shoes in the country. A pair of pre-First World War Lobb riding boots given to him by 'a marvellous old boulevardier and *screaming* queen who was rather a friend of my father's' were only brought out on special occasions when the subject of boots or shoes arose spontaneously in the conversation.

He was driving Ali Montague down to the Bossington-Lanes', where they were both staying. Ali, who had known Bill Bossington-Lane for forty years, had described him and his wife as 'the sort of people one never sees in London. They just don't travel well.'

Someone once asked Bill if he still had his beautiful

manor house. 'Beautiful manor house?' he said. 'We've still got the old dump, if that's what you mean.' 'By the way,' Ali continued, 'did you see that thing in Dempster about tonight? After all the usual rubbish about the best shoot in England, and ten thousand acres and Princess Margaret, there was Bridget saying, "I'm just having a few people round to celebrate my husband's birthday." She just can't get it right, can she?'

'Ugh,' groaned Alexander, 'I can't stand that woman. I mean, I almost don't mind being patronized by Princess Margaret, and no doubt will be tonight—'

'You should be so lucky,' interjected Ali. 'Do you know, I think I *prefer* parties given by people I don't like.'

'But,' Alexander continued, unperturbed, 'I won't be patronized by Bridget Gravesend, née Watson-Spot or whatever it was.'

'Watson-Spot,' laughed Ali. 'Oddly enough I knew the father *slightly* in another lifetime. He was called Roddy Watson-Scott, frightfully stupid and jolly and rather used-car salesman, but nice. As you know I'm *not* a snob, but you didn't have to be a snob to drop that man.'

'Well, there you are,' said Politsky. 'I don't want to be patronized by the daughter of a used-car salesman. After all, my family used to be able to walk from Moscow to Kiev on their own land.'

'It's no use telling me about these foreign places,' said Ali. 'I'm afraid I just don't know where Kiev is.'

'All you need to know is that it's a very long way from Moscow,' said Alexander curtly. 'Anyway, it sounds as if Bridget'll get her comeuppance with this Cindy Smith affair.'

'What I can't understand is why Cindy's gone for Sonny,' said Ali.

'He's the key to the world she wants to penetrate.'

'Or be penetrated *by*,' said Ali.

Both men smiled.

'By the way, are you wearing pumps this evening?' asked Alexander casually.

With her fist, Anne Eisen rubbed the Jaguar's back window and got nowhere; the dirty fog on the other side stood its ground.

The driver glanced in the rear-view mirror disapprovingly.

'Do you know where we are?' asked Tom.

'Sure,' said Anne. 'We're out of our minds.' She

spaced the words slowly and evenly. 'That's where we are. We're on our way to see a lot of museum pieces, arrogant snobs, airheads, and feudal boondockers . . .'

'Harold tells me that Princess Margaret is coming.'

'And thick Krauts.' Anne added this last item to her list with satisfaction.

The Jaguar turned left and crept down to the end of a long drive where the lights of an Elizabethan manor glowed through the fog. They had arrived at Harold Greene's, their host for the weekend.

'Wow!' said Anne. 'Get a load of this: fifty rooms, and I'll bet all of them are haunted.'

Tom, picking up a battered leather case from the floor, was not impressed. 'It's a Harold-type house,' he said, 'I'll give you that. He had one just like it years ago in Arlington, when we were young and saving the world.'

6

Bridget had told her mother to get a taxi at the station and not to worry because she would pay, but when Virginia Watson-Scott arrived at Cheatley she was too embarrassed to ask and so she paid herself, although seventeen pounds plus a pound for the driver was no small sum.

'If orchids could write novels,' Tony Fowles was saying when Virginia was shown into Bridget's little sitting room, 'they would write novels like Isabel's.'

'Oh, hello, Mummy,' sighed Bridget, getting up from the sofa where she'd been drinking in Tony's words. The Valium had helped to muffle the impact of overhearing Sonny's telephone call, and Bridget was slightly shocked but pleased by her ability to enter into the trance of habit and to be distracted by Tony's witty conversation. Nevertheless the presence of her mother struck her as an additional and unfair burden.

'I thought I was so well organized,' she explained to her mother, 'but I've still got a million and one things to do. Do you know Tony Fowles?'

Tony got up and shook hands. 'Pleased to meet you,' he said.

'It's nice to be in proper countryside,' said Virginia, nervous of silence. 'It's become so built-up around me.'

'I know,' said Tony. 'I love seeing cows, don't you? They're so natural.'

'Oh yes,' said Virginia, 'cows are nice.'

'My trouble,' Tony confessed, 'is that I'm so aesthetic. I want to rush into the field and arrange them. Then I'd have them glued to the spot so they looked perfect from the house.'

'Poor cows,' said Virginia, 'I don't think they'd like that. Where's Belinda?' she asked Bridget.

'In the nursery, I imagine,' said Bridget. 'It's a bit early, but would you like some tea?'

'I'd rather see Belinda first,' Virginia replied, remembering that Bridget had asked her to come at teatime.

'All right, we'll go and have tea in the nursery,' said

Bridget. 'I'm afraid your room is on the nursery floor anyhow – we're so crowded with Princess Margaret and everything – so I can show you your room at the same time.'

'Righty-ho,' said Virginia. It was a phrase Roddy had always used, and it drove Bridget mad.

'Oh,' she couldn't help groaning, 'please don't use that expression.'

'I must have caught it from Roddy!'

'I know,' said Bridget. She could picture her father in his blazer and his cavalry twills saying 'righty-ho' as he put on his driving gloves. He had always been kind to her, but once she had learned to be embarrassed by him she had never stopped, even after he died.

'Let's go up, then,' sighed Bridget. 'You'll come with us, won't you?' she pleaded with Tony.

'Aye-aye,' said Tony, saluting, 'or aren't I allowed to say that?'

Bridget led the way to the nursery. Nanny, who had been in the middle of scolding Belinda for being 'overexcited', set off to make tea in the nursery kitchen, muttering, 'Both parents in one day,' with a mixture of awe and resentment.

'Granny!' said Belinda, who liked her grandmother. 'I didn't know you were coming!'

'Didn't anyone tell you?' asked Virginia, too pleased with Belinda to dwell on this oversight.

Tony and Bridget moved over to the tattered old sofa at the far end of the room.

'Roses,' said Tony reproachfully, sitting down.

'Aren't they sweet together?' asked Bridget, watching Belinda on Virginia's knee, peering into her grandmother's bag to see if there were sweets in it. For a moment Bridget could remember being in the same position and feeling happy.

'Sweet,' confirmed Tony, 'or sweets anyway.'

'You old cynic,' said Bridget.

Tony put on an expression of wounded innocence. 'I'm not a cynic,' he moaned. 'Is it my fault that most people are motivated by greed and envy?'

'What motivates you?' asked Bridget.

'Style,' said Tony bashfully. 'And love for my friends,' he added, softly patting Bridget's wrist.

'Don't try to butter me up,' said Bridget.

'Who's being a cynic now?' gasped Tony.

'Look what Granny brought me,' said Belinda, holding out a bag of lemon sherbets, her favourite sweets.

'Would you like one?' she asked her mother.

'You mustn't give her sweets,' said Bridget to Virginia. 'They're frightfully bad for her teeth.'

'I only bought a quarter of a pound,' said Virginia. 'You used to like them too as a girl.'

'Nanny disapproves terribly, don't you, Nanny?' asked Bridget, taking advantage of the reappearance of Nanny with a tea tray.

'Oh yes,' said Nanny, who hadn't in fact heard what was being discussed.

'Sweets rot little girls' teeth,' said Bridget.

'Sweets!' cried Nanny, able to focus on the enemy at last. 'No sweets in the nursery except on Sundays!' she thundered.

Belinda ran through the nursery door and out into the corridor. 'I'm not in the nursery anymore,' she chanted.

Virginia put her hand over her mouth to make a show of concealing her laughter. 'I didn't want to cause any trouble,' she said.

'Oh, she's a lively one,' said Nanny cunningly, seeing that Bridget secretly admired Belinda's rebelliousness.

Virginia followed Belinda out into the corridor. Tony looked critically at the old tweed skirt she wore.

Stylish it was not. He felt licensed by Bridget's attitude to despise Virginia, without forgoing the pleasure of despising Bridget for not being more loyal to her mother, or stylish enough to rise above her.

'You should take your mum shopping for a new skirt,' he suggested.

'Don't be so rude,' said Bridget.

Tony could smell the weakness in her indignation. 'That maroon check gives me a headache,' he insisted.

'It is ghastly,' admitted Bridget.

Nanny brought over two cups of tea, and a plate of Jaffa Cakes.

'Granny's going to keep the sweets for me,' said Belinda, coming back into the nursery. 'And I have to ask her if I want one.'

'It seemed to us like a good compromise,' Virginia explained.

'And she's going to read me a story before dinner,' said Belinda.

'Oh, I meant to tell you,' said Bridget absently, 'you've been asked to dinner at the Bossington-Lanes'. I couldn't refuse, they made such a fuss about needing extra women. It'll be so stuffy here with Princess Margaret, you'll be much more at home over there. They're neighbours of ours, frightfully nice.'

'Oh,' said Virginia. 'Well, if I'm needed I suppose . . .'

'You don't *mind*, do you?' asked Bridget.

'Oh no,' said Virginia.

'I mean, I thought it would be nicer for you, more relaxed.'

'Yes, I'm sure I'll be more relaxed,' said Virginia.

'I mean, if you really don't want to go I could still cancel them I suppose, although they'll be frightfully angry at this stage.'

'No, no,' said Virginia. 'I'd love to go, you mustn't cancel them now. They sound very nice. Will you excuse me a moment?' she added, getting up and opening the door that led to the other rooms on the nursery floor.

'Did I handle that all right?' Bridget asked Tony.

'You deserve an Oscar.'

'You don't think it was unkind of me? It's just that I don't think I can handle P.M. and Sonny *and* my mother all at once.'

'You did the right thing,' Tony reassured her. 'After all, you couldn't very well send either of *those* two to the Bossington-Lanes'.'

'I know, but I mean, I was thinking of her too.'

'I'm sure she'll be happier there,' said Tony. 'She

seems a nice woman but she's not very . . .' he searched for the right word, '. . . social, is she?'

'No,' said Bridget. 'I know the whole P.M. thing would make her terribly tense.'

'Is Granny upset?' asked Belinda, coming to sit down next to her mother.

'What on earth makes you ask that?'

'She looked sad when she left.'

'That's just the way she looks when her face relaxes,' said Bridget inventively.

Virginia came back into the nursery, stuffing her handkerchief up the sleeve of her cardigan.

'I went into one of the rooms for a moment and saw my suitcase there,' she said cheerfully. 'Is that where I'm sleeping?'

'Hmm,' said Bridget, picking up her cup of tea and sipping it slowly. 'I'm sorry it's rather poky, but after all it's only for one night.'

'Just for one night,' echoed Virginia, who'd been hoping to stay for two or three.

'The house is incredibly full,' said Bridget. 'It's such a strain on . . . on everybody.' She tactfully swallowed the word 'servants' in Nanny's presence. 'Anyhow, I thought you'd like to be near Belinda.'

'Oh, of course,' said Virginia. 'We can have a midnight feast.'

'A midnight feast,' spluttered Nanny who could contain herself no longer. 'Not in *my* nursery!'

'I thought it was Belinda's nursery,' said Tony waspishly.

'I'm in charge,' gasped Nanny, 'and I can't have midnight feasts.'

Bridget could remember the midnight feast her mother had made to cheer her up on the night before she went to boarding school. Her mother had pretended that they had to hide from her father, but Bridget later found out that he had known all about it and had even gone to buy the cakes himself. She suppressed this sentimental memory with a sigh and got up when she heard the noise of cars at the front of the house. She craned out of one of the small windows in the corner of the nursery.

'Oh God, it's the Alantours,' she said. 'I suppose I have to go down and say hello to them. Tony, will you be an angel and help me?' she asked.

'As long as you leave me time to put on my ball gown for Princess Margaret,' said Tony.

'Can I do anything?' asked Virginia.

'No, thanks. You stay here and unpack. I'll order

you a taxi to go to the Bossington-Lanes'. At about seven thirty,' said Bridget calculating that Princess Margaret would not yet have come down for a drink. 'My treat, of course,' she added.

Oh, dear, thought Virginia, more money down the drain.

7

Patrick had booked his room late and so had been put in the annexe of the Little Soddington House Hotel. With the letter confirming his reservation the management had enclosed a brochure featuring a vast room with a four-poster bed, a tall marble fireplace, and a bay window opening onto wide views of the ravishing Cotswolds. The room Patrick was shown into, with its severely pitched ceiling and view onto the kitchen yard, boasted a full complement of tea-making facilities, instant-coffee sachets, and tiny pots of longlife milk. The miniature floral pattern on its matching waste-paper basket, curtains, bedspread, cushions, and Kleenex dispenser seemed to shift and shimmer.

Patrick unpacked his dinner jacket and threw it onto the bed, throwing himself down after it. A notice under the glass of the bedside table said: 'To avoid disappointment, residents are advised to book in the restaurant in advance.' Patrick, who had been trying to avoid disappointment all his life, cursed himself for not discovering this formula earlier.

Was there no other way he could stop being disappointed? How could he find any firm ground when his identity seemed to begin with disintegration and go on to disintegrate further? But perhaps this whole model of identity was misconceived. Perhaps identity was not a building for which one had to find foundations, but rather a series of impersonations held together by a central intelligence, an intelligence that knew the history of the impersonations and eliminated the distinction between action and acting.

'Impersonation, sir,' grunted Patrick, thrusting out his stomach and waddling towards the bathroom, as if he were the Fat Man himself, 'is a habit of which I cannot approve, it was the ruination of Monsieur Escoffier . . .' He stopped.

The self-disgust that afflicted him these days had the stagnancy of a malarial swamp, and he sometimes missed the cast of jeering characters that had accompanied the more dramatic disintegrations of his early twenties. Although he could conjure up some of these characters, they seemed to have lost their energy, just as he had soon forgotten the agony of being a ventriloquist's dummy and replaced it with a sense of nostalgia for a period that had made up for some of its unpleasantness with its intensity.

'Be absolute for death', a strange phrase from *Measure for Measure*, returned to him while he bared his teeth to rip open a sachet of bath gel. Perhaps there was something in this half-shallow, half-profound idea that one had to despair of life in order to grasp its real value. Then again, perhaps there wasn't. But in any case, he pondered, squeezing the green slime from the sachet and trying to get back to his earlier line of thought, what was this central intelligence, and just how intelligent was it? What was the thread that held together the scattered beads of experience if not the pressure of interpretation? The meaning of life was whatever meaning one could thrust down its reluctant throat.

Where was Victor Eisen, the great philosopher, when he needed him most? How could he have left the doubtless splendid *Being, Knowing, and Judging* (or was it *Thinking, Knowing, and Judging*?) behind in New York when Anne Eisen had generously given him a copy during his corpse-collecting trip?

On his most recent visit to New York, he'd been back

to the funeral parlour where, years before, he had seen his father's body. The building was not as he remembered it at all. Instead of the grey stone facade, he saw soft brown brick. The building was much smaller than he expected and when he was driven inside by curiosity he found that there was no chequered black-and-white marble floor, and no reception desk where he expected to see one. Perhaps it had been changed, but even so, the scale was wrong, like places remembered from childhood and dwarfed by the passage of time.

The strange thing was that Patrick refused to alter his memory of the funeral parlour. He found the picture he had evolved over the years more compelling than the facts with which he was presented on revisiting the place. This picture was more suitable to the events that had occurred within the disappointing building. What he must remain true to was the effort of interpretation, the thread on which he tried to hang the scattered beads.

Even involuntary memory was only the resurfacing of an old story, something that had definitely once been a story. Impressions that were too fleeting to be called stories yielded no meaning. On the same visit to New York he had passed a red-and-white funnel next to some roadworks, spewing steam into the cold air. It felt nostalgic and significant, but left him in a state of nebulous intensity, not knowing whether he was remembering an image from a film, a book, or his own life. On the same walk he had dropped into a sleazy hotel in which he had once lived and found that it was no longer a hotel. The thing he was remembering no longer existed but, blind to the refurbished lobby, he continued to imagine the Italian with the scimitar tie-pin accusing him of trying to install his girlfriend Natasha as a prostitute, and to imagine the frenetic wallpaper covered in scratchy red lines like the frayed blood vessels of exhausted eyes.

What could he do but accept the disturbing extent to which memory was fictional and hope that the fiction lay at the service of a truth less richly represented by the original facts?

The house in Lacoste, where Patrick had spent most of his childhood, was now separated by only a few vines from a nasty suburb. Its old furniture had been sold and the redundant well filled in and sealed. Even the tree frogs, bright green and smooth against the smooth grey bark of the fig trees, had gone, poisoned, or deprived of their breeding ground. Standing on the cracked terrace, listening to the whining of a new motorway, Patrick would try to hallucinate the faces that used to emerge from the smoky fluidity of the limestone crags, but they remained stubbornly hidden. On the other hand, geckos still flickered over the ceilings and under the eaves of the roof, and a tremor of unresolved violence always disturbed the easy atmosphere of holidays, like the churning of an engine setting the gin trembling on a distant deck. Some things never let him down.

The phone rang, and Patrick picked it up hastily, grateful for the interruption. It was Johnny saying that he'd arrived, and suggesting that they meet in the bar at eight thirty. Patrick agreed and, released from the hamster's wheel of his thoughts, got up to turn off the bathwater.

David Windfall, florid and hot from his bath, squeezed into dinner jacket trousers that seemed to strain like sausage skins from the pressure of his thighs. Beads of sweat broke out continually on his upper lip and forehead. He wiped them away, glancing at himself in the mirror; although he looked like a hippopotamus with hypertension he was well satisfied.

He was going to have dinner with Cindy Smith. She was world-famously sexy and glamorous, but David was not intimidated because he was charming and sophisticated and, well, English. The Windfalls had been making their influence felt in Cumbria for centuries before Miss Smith popped onto the scene, he reassured himself as he buttoned up the overtight shirt on his already sweating neck. His wife was in the habit of buying him seventeen-and-a-half-inch collars in the hope that he would grow thin enough to wear them. This trick made him so indignant that he decided that she deserved to be ill and absent and, if everything went well, betrayed.

He still hadn't told Mrs Bossington-Lane that he wouldn't be going to her dinner. He decided, as he choked himself on his bow tie, that the best way to handle it was to seek her out at the party and claim that his car had broken down. He just hoped that nobody else he knew would be having dinner in the hotel. He might try to use this fear to persuade Cindy to dine in his room. His thoughts panted on optimistically.

It was Cindy Smith who occupied the magnificent bedroom advertised in the brochure of the hotel. They'd told her it was a suite, but it was just a semi-large bedroom without a separate seating area. These old English houses were so uncomfortable. She'd only seen a photograph of Cheatley from the outside, and it looked real big, but there'd better be underfloor heating and a whole lot of private bathrooms, or she couldn't even face her own plan to become the independently wealthy ex-Countess of Gravesend.

She was taking a long-term view and looking ahead two or three years. Looks didn't last forever and she wasn't ready for religion yet. Money was kind of a good compromise, staked up somewhere between cosmetics and eternity. Besides, she liked Sonny, she really did. He was cute, not to look at, God no, but aristocratic cute, old-fashioned out-of-a-movie cute.

Last year in Paris all the other models had come back to her suite in the Lotti – now there was a real suite – and each one of them, except a couple who chickened out, had done her fake orgasm, and Cindy's was voted Best Fake Orgasm. They'd pretended the champagne bottle was an Oscar and she'd made an acceptance speech thanking all the men without whom it wouldn't have been possible. Too bad she'd mentioned Sonny, seeing how she was going to marry him. Whoops!

She'd drunk a bit too much and put her father on the list also, which was probably a mistake 'cause all the other girls fell silent and things weren't so much fun after that.

Patrick arrived downstairs before Johnny, and ordered a glass of Perrier at the bar. Two middle-aged couples sat together at a nearby table. The only other person in the bar, a florid man in a dinner jacket, obviously going to Sonny's party, sat with folded arms, looking towards the door.

Patrick took his drink over to a small book-lined alcove in the corner of the room. Scanning the shelves, his eye fell on a volume called *The Journal of a Disappointed Man*, and next to it a second volume called *More Journals of a Disappointed Man*, and finally, by the same author, a third volume entitled *Enjoying Life*. How could a man who had made such a promising start to his career have ended up writing a book called *Enjoying Life*? Patrick took the offending volume from the shelf and read the first sentence that he saw: 'Verily, the flight of a gull is as magnificent as the Andes!'

'Verily,' murmured Patrick.

'Hi.'

'Hello, Johnny,' said Patrick, looking up from the page. 'I've just found a book called *Enjoying Life*.'

'Intriguing,' said Johnny, sitting down on the other side of the alcove.

'I'm going to take it to my room and read it tomorrow. It might save my life. Mind you, I don't know why people get so fixated on happiness, which always eludes them, when there are so many other invigorating experiences available, like rage, jealousy, disgust, and so forth.'

'Don't you want to be happy?' asked Johnny.

'Well, when you put it like *that*,' smiled Patrick.

'Really you're just like everyone else.'

'Don't push your luck,' Patrick warned him.

'Will you be dining with us this evening, gentlemen?' asked a waiter.

'Yes,' replied Johnny, taking a menu, and passing one on to Patrick who was too deep in the alcove for the waiter to reach.

'I thought he said, "Will you be dying with us?"' admitted Patrick, who was feeling increasingly uneasy about his decision to tell Johnny the facts he had kept secret for thirty years.

'Maybe he did,' said Johnny. 'We haven't read the menu yet.'

'I suppose "the young" will be taking drugs tonight,' sighed Patrick, scanning the menu.

'Ecstasy: the non-addictive high,' said Johnny.

'Call me old fashioned,' blustered Patrick, 'but I don't like the sound of a non-addictive drug.'

Johnny felt frustratingly engulfed in his old style of banter with Patrick. These were just the sort of 'old associations' that he was supposed to sever, but what could he do? Patrick was a great friend and he wanted him to be less miserable.

'Why do you think we're so discontented?' asked Johnny, settling for the smoked salmon.

'I don't know,' lied Patrick. 'I can't decide between the onion soup and the traditional English goat's cheese salad. An analyst once told me I was suffering from a "depression on top of a depression".'

'Well, at least you got on top of the first depression,' said Johnny, closing the menu.

'Exactly,' smiled Patrick. 'I don't think one can improve on the traitor of Strasbourg whose last request was that he give the order to the firing squad himself. Christ! Look at that girl!' he burst out in a half-mournful surge of excitement.

'It's whatshername, the model.'

'Oh, yeah. Well, at least now I can get obsessed with an unobtainable fuck,' said Patrick. 'Obsession dispels depression: the third law of psychodynamics.'

'What are the others?'

'That people loathe those they've wronged, and that they despise the victims of misfortune, and . . . I'll think of some more over dinner.'

'I don't despise the victims of misfortune,' said Johnny. 'I am worried that misfortune is contagious, but I'm not secretly convinced that it's deserved.'

'Look at her,' said Patrick, 'pacing around the cage of her Valentino dress, longing to be released into her natural habitat.'

'Calm down,' said Johnny, 'she's probably frigid.'

'Just as well if she is,' said Patrick. 'I haven't had sex for so long I can't remember what it's like, except that it takes place in that distant grey zone beneath the neck.'

'It's not grey.'

'Well, there you are, I can't even remember what it looks like, but I sometimes think it would be nice to have a relationship with my body which wasn't based on illness or addiction.'

'What about work and love?' asked Johnny.

'You know it's not fair to ask me about work,' said Patrick reproachfully, 'but my experience of love is that you get excited thinking that someone can mend your broken heart, and then you get angry when you realize that they can't. A certain economy creeps into the process and the jewelled daggers that used to pierce one's heart are replaced by ever-blunter penknives.'

'Did you expect Debbie to mend your broken heart?'

'Of course, but we were like two people taking turns with a bandage – I'm afraid to say that her turns tended to be a great deal shorter. I don't blame anyone anymore – I always mostly and rightly blamed myself . . .' Patrick stopped. 'It's just sad to spend so long getting to know someone and explaining yourself to them, and then having no use for the knowledge.'

'Do you prefer being sad to being bitter?' asked Johnny.

'Marginally,' said Patrick. 'It took me some time to get bitter. I used to think I saw things clearly when we were going out. I thought, she's a mess and I'm a mess, but at least I know what kind of mess I am.'

'Big deal,' said Johnny.

'Quite,' sighed Patrick. 'One seldom knows whether perseverance is noble or stupid until it's too late. Most people either feel regret at staying with someone for too long, or regret at losing them too easily. I manage to feel both ways at the same time about the same object.'

'Congratulations,' said Johnny.

Patrick raised his hands, as if trying to quiet the roar of applause.

'But why is your heart broken?' asked Johnny, struck by Patrick's unguarded manner.

'Some women,' said Patrick, ignoring the question, 'provide you with anaesthetic, if you're lucky, or a mirror in which you can watch yourself making clumsy incisions, but most of them spend their time tearing open old wounds.' Patrick took a gulp of Perrier. 'Listen,' he said, 'there's something I want to tell you.'

'Your table is ready, gentlemen,' a waiter announced with gusto. 'If you'd care to follow me into the dining room.'

Johnny and Patrick got up and followed him into a brown-carpeted dining room decorated with portraits of sunlit salmon and bonneted squires' wives, each table flickering with the light of a single pink candle.

Patrick loosened his bow tie and undid the top button of his shirt. How could he tell Johnny? How could he tell anyone? But if he told no one, he would stay endlessly isolated and divided against himself.

He knew that under the tall grass of an apparently untamed future the steel rails of fear and habit were already laid. What he suddenly couldn't bear, with every cell in his body, was to act out the destiny prepared for him by his past, and slide obediently along those rails, contemplating bitterly all the routes he would rather have taken.

But which words could he use? All his life he'd used words to distract attention from this deep inarticulacy, this unspeakable emotion which he would now have to use words to describe. How could they avoid being noisy and tactless, like a gaggle of children laughing under the bedroom window of a dying man? And wouldn't he rather tell a woman, and be engulfed in maternal solicitude, or scorched by sexual frenzy? Yes, yes, yes. Or a psychiatrist, to whom he would be almost obliged to make such an offering, although he had resisted the temptation often enough. Or his mother, that Mrs Jellyby whose telescopic philanthropy had saved so many Ethiopian orphans while her own child fell into the fire. And yet Patrick wanted to tell an unpaid witness, without money, without sex, and without blame, just another human being. Perhaps he should tell the waiter: at least he wouldn't be seeing him again.

'There's something I have to tell you,' he repeated, after they had sat down and ordered their food. Johnny paused expectantly, putting down his glass of water from an intuition that he had better not be gulping or munching during the next few minutes.

'It's not that I'm embarrassed,' Patrick mumbled. 'It's more a question of not wanting to burden you with something you can't really be expected to do anything about.'

'Go ahead,' said Johnny.

'I know that I've told you about my parents' divorce and the drunkenness and the violence and the fecklessness . . . That's not really the point at all. What I was skirting around and not saying is that when I was five—'

'Here we are, gentlemen,' said the waiter, bringing the first courses with a flourish.

'Thank you,' said Johnny. 'Go on.'

Patrick waited for the waiter to slip away. He must try to be as simple as he could.

'When I was five, my father "abused" me, as we're invited to call it these days—' Patrick suddenly broke off in silence, unable to sustain the casualness he'd been labouring to achieve. Switchblades of memory that had flashed open all his life reappeared and silenced him.

'How do you mean "abused"?' asked Johnny uncertainly. The answer somehow became clear as he formulated the question.

'I . . .' Patrick couldn't speak. The crumpled bedspread with the blue phoenixes, the pool of cold slime at the base of his spine, scuttling off over the tiles. These were memories he was not prepared to talk about.

He picked up his fork and stuck the prongs discreetly but very hard into the underside of his wrist, trying to force himself back into the present and the conversational responsibilities he was neglecting.

'It was . . .' he sighed, concussed by memory.

After having watched Patrick drawl his way fluently through every crisis, Johnny was shocked at seeing him unable to speak, and he found his eyes glazed with a film of tears. 'I'm so sorry,' he murmured.

'Nobody should do that to anybody else,' said Patrick, almost whispering.

'Is everything to your satisfaction, gentlemen?' said the chirpy waiter.

'Look, do you think you could leave us alone for

five minutes so we can have a conversation?' snapped Patrick, suddenly regaining his voice.

'I'm sorry, sir,' said the waiter archly.

'I can't stand this fucking music,' said Patrick, glancing around the dining room aggressively. Subdued Chopin teetered familiarly on the edge of hearing.

'Why don't they turn the fucking thing off, or turn it up?' he snarled. 'What do I mean by abused?' he added impatiently. 'I mean sexually abused.'

'God, I'm sorry,' said Johnny. 'I'd always wondered why you hated your father quite so much.'

'Well, now you know. The first incident masqueraded as a punishment. It had a certain Kafkaesque charm: the crime was never named and therefore took on great generality and intensity.'

'Did this go on?' asked Johnny.

'Yes, yes,' said Patrick hastily.

'What a bastard,' said Johnny.

'That's what I've been saying for years,' said Patrick. 'But now I'm exhausted by hating him. I can't go on. The hatred binds me to those events and I don't want to be a child anymore.' Patrick was back in the vein again, released from silence by the habits of analysis and speculation.

'It must have split the world in half for you,' said Johnny.

Patrick was taken aback by the precision of this comment.

'Yes. Yes, I think that's exactly what happened. How did you know?'

'It seemed pretty obvious.'

'It's strange to hear someone say that it's obvious. It always seemed to me so secret and complicated.' Patrick paused. He felt that although what he was saying mattered to him enormously, there was a core of inarticulacy that he hadn't attacked at all. His intellect could only generate more distinctions or define the distinctions better.

'I always thought the truth would set me free,' he said, 'but the truth just drives you mad.'

'Telling the truth might set you free.'

'Maybe. But self-knowledge on its own is useless.'

'Well, it enables you to suffer more lucidly,' argued Johnny.

'Oh, ya, I wouldn't miss that for the world.'

'In the end perhaps the only way to alleviate misery is to become more detached about yourself and more attached to something else,' said Johnny.

'Are you suggesting I take up a hobby?' laughed Patrick. 'Weaving baskets or sewing mailbags?'

'Well, actually, I was trying to think of a way to avoid those two particular occupations,' said Johnny.

'But if I were released from my bitter and unpleasant state of mind,' protested Patrick, 'what would be left?'

'Nothing much,' admitted Johnny, 'but think what you could put there instead.'

'You're making me dizzy . . . Oddly enough there was something about hearing the word mercy in *Measure for Measure* last night that made me imagine there might be a course that is neither bitter nor false, something that lies beyond argument. But if there is I can't grasp it; all I know is that I'm tired of having these steel brushes whirring around the inside of my skull.'

Both men paused while the waiter silently cleared away their plates. Patrick was puzzled by how easy it had been to tell another person the most shameful and secret truth about his life. And yet he felt dissatisfied; the catharsis of confession eluded him. Perhaps he had been too abstract. His 'father' had become the code-name for a set of his own psychological difficulties and he had forgotten the real man, with his grey curls and his wheezing chest and his proud face, who had made such clumsy efforts in his closing years to endear himself to those he had betrayed.

When Eleanor had finally gathered the courage to divorce David, he had gone into a decline. Like a disgraced torturer whose victim has died, he cursed himself for not pacing his cruelty better, guilt and self-pity competing for mastery of his mood. David had the further frustration of being defied by Patrick who, at the age of eight, inspired by his parents' separation, refused one day to give in to his father's sexual assaults. Patrick's transformation of himself from a toy into a person shattered his father, who realized that Patrick must have known what was being done to him.

During this difficult time, David went to visit Nicholas Pratt in Sister Agnes, where he was recovering from a painful operation on his intestine following the failure of his fourth marriage. David, reeling from the prospect of his own divorce, found Nicholas lying in bed drinking champagne smuggled in by loyal friends, and only too ready to discuss how one should never trust a bloody woman.

'I want someone to design me a fortress,' said David, for whom Eleanor was proposing to build a small house surprisingly close to her own house in

Lacoste. 'I don't want to look out on the fucking world again.'

'Completely understand,' slurred Nicholas, whose speech had become at once thicker and more staccato in his post-operative haze. 'Only trouble with the bloody world is the bloody people in it,' he said. 'Give me that writing paper, would you?'

While David paced up and down the room, flouting the hospital rules by smoking a cigar, Nicholas, who liked to surprise his friends with his amateur draughtsmanship, made a sketch worthy of David's misanthropic ecstasy.

'Keep the buggers out,' he said when he had finished, tossing the page across the bedclothes.

David picked it up and saw a pentagonal house with no windows on the outside and a central courtyard in which Nicholas had poetically planted a cypress tree, flaring above the low roof like a black flame.

The architect who was given this sketch took pity on David and introduced a single window into the exterior wall of the drawing room. David locked the shutters and stuffed crunched-up copies of *The Times* into the aperture, cursing himself for not sacking the architect when he first visited him in his disastrously converted farmhouse near Aix, with its algae-choked swimming pool. He pressed the window closed on the newspaper and then sealed it with the thick black tape favoured by those who wish to gas themselves efficiently. Finally a curtain was drawn across the window and only reopened by rare visitors who were soon made aware of their error by David's rage.

The cypress tree never flourished and its twisted trunk and grey peeling bark writhed in a dismal parody of Nicholas's noble vision. Nicholas himself, after designing the house, was too busy ever to accept an invitation. 'One doesn't have fun with David Melrose these days,' he would tell people in London. This was a polite way to describe the state of mental illness into which David had degenerated. Woken every night by his own screaming nightmares, he lay in bed almost continuously for seven years, wearing those yellow-and-white flannel pyjamas, now worn through at the elbows, which were the only things he had inherited from his father, thanks to the generous intervention of his mother who had refused to see him leave the funeral empty-handed. The most enthusiastic thing he could do was to smoke a cigar, a habit his father had first encouraged in him, and one he had passed on to Patrick, among so many other disadvantages, like a baton thrust from one wheezing generation to the next. If David left his house he was dressed like a tramp, muttering to himself in giant supermarkets on the outskirts of Marseilles. Sometimes in winter he wandered about the house in dark glasses, trailing a Japanese dressing gown, and clutching a glass of pastis, checking again and again that the heating was off so that he didn't waste any money. The contempt that saved him from complete madness drove him almost completely mad. When he emerged from his depression he was a ghost, not improved but diminished, trying to tempt people to stay in the house that had been designed to repel their unlikely invasion.

Patrick stayed in this house during his adolescence, sitting in the courtyard, shooting olive stones over the roof so that they at least could be free. His arguments with his father, or rather his one interminable argument, reached a crucial point when Patrick said something more fundamentally insulting to David than David had just said to him, and David, conscious that he was growing slower and weaker while his son grew faster and nastier, reached into his pocket for his heart pills and, shaking them into his tortured rheumatic hands, said with a melancholy whisper, 'You mustn't say those things to your old Dad.'

Patrick's triumph was tainted by the guilty conviction that his father was about to die of a heart attack. Still, things were not the same after that, especially when Patrick was able to patronize his disinherited father with a small income, and cheapen him with his money as Eleanor had once cheapened him with hers. During those closing years Patrick's terror had largely been eclipsed by pity, and also by boredom in the company of his 'poor old Dad'. He had sometimes dreamed that they might have an honest conversation, but a moment in his father's company made it clear that this would never happen. And yet Patrick felt there was something missing, something he wasn't admitting to himself, let alone telling Johnny.

Respecting Patrick's silence, Johnny had eaten his way through most of his corn-fed chicken by the time Patrick spoke again.

'So, what can one say about a man who rapes his own child?'

'I suppose it might help if you could see him as sick rather than evil,' Johnny suggested limply. 'I can't get over this,' he added, 'it's really awful.'

'I've tried what you suggest,' said Patrick, 'but then, what is evil if not sickness celebrating itself? While my father had any power he showed no remorse or restraint, and when he was poor and abandoned he only showed contempt and morbidity.'

'Maybe you can see his actions as evil, but see *him* as sick. Maybe one can't condemn another person, only their actions . . .' Johnny hesitated, reluctant to take on the role of the defence. 'Maybe he couldn't stop himself anymore than you could stop yourself taking drugs.'

'Maybe, maybe, maybe,' said Patrick, 'but I didn't harm anyone else by taking drugs.'

'Really? What about Debbie?'

'She was a grown-up, she could choose. I certainly gave her a hard time,' Patrick admitted. 'I don't know, I try to negotiate truces of one sort or another, but then I run up against this unnegotiable rage.' Patrick pushed his plate back and lit a cigarette. 'I don't want any pudding, do you?'

'No, just coffee.'

'Two coffees, please,' said Patrick to the waiter who was now theatrically tight-lipped. 'I'm sorry I snapped at you earlier, I was in the middle of trying to say something rather tricky.'

'I was only trying to do my job,' said the waiter.

'Of course,' said Patrick.

'Do you think there's any way you can forgive him?' asked Johnny.

'Oh, yes,' said the waiter, 'it wasn't that bad.'

'No, not you,' laughed Johnny.

'Sorry I spoke,' said the waiter, going off to fetch the coffee.

'Your father, I mean.'

'Well, if that absurd waiter can forgive me, who knows what chain reaction of absolution might not be set in motion?' said Patrick. 'But then neither revenge nor forgiveness change what happened. They're sideshows, of which forgiveness is the less attractive because it represents a collaboration with one's persecutors. I don't suppose that forgiveness was uppermost in the minds of people who were being nailed to a cross until Jesus, if not the first man with a Christ complex still the most successful, wafted onto the scene. Presumably those who enjoyed inflicting cruelty could hardly believe their luck and set about popularizing the superstition that their victims could only achieve peace of mind by forgiving them.'

'You don't think it might be a profound spiritual truth?' asked Johnny.

Patrick puffed out his cheeks. 'I suppose it might be, but as far as I'm concerned, what is meant to show the spiritual advantages of forgiveness in fact shows the psychological advantages of thinking you're the son of God.'

'So how do you get free?' asked Johnny.

'Search me,' said Patrick. 'Obviously, or I wouldn't have told you, I think it has something to do with telling the truth. I'm only at the beginning, but presumably there comes a point when you grow bored of telling it, and that point coincides with your "freedom".'

'So rather than forgive you're going to try and talk it out.'

'Yes, narrative fatigue is what I'm going for. If the talk cure is our modern religion then narrative fatigue must be its apotheosis,' said Patrick suavely.

'But the truth includes an understanding of your father.'

'I couldn't understand my father better and I still don't like what he did.'

'Of course you don't. Perhaps there is nothing to say except, "What a bastard." I was only groping for an alternative because you said you were exhausted by hatred.'

'I am, but at the moment I can't imagine any kind of liberation except eventual indifference.'

'Or detachment,' said Johnny. 'I don't suppose you'll ever be indifferent.'

'Yes, detachment,' said Patrick, who didn't mind having his vocabulary corrected on this occasion. 'Indifference just sounded cooler.'

The two men drank their coffee, Johnny feeling that he had been drawn too far away from Patrick's original revelation to ask, 'What actually happened?'

Patrick, for his part, suspected that he had left the soil of his own experience, where wasps still gnawed at the gaping figs and he stared down madly onto his own five-year-old head, in order to avoid an uneasiness that lay even deeper than the uneasiness of his confession. The roots of his imagination were in the Pagan South and the unseemly liberation it had engendered in his father, but the discussion had somehow remained in the Cotswolds being dripped on by the ghosts of England's rude elms. The opportunity to make a grand gesture and say, 'This thing of darkness I acknowledge mine,' had somehow petered out into ethical debate.

'Thanks for telling me what you've told me,' said Johnny.

'No need to get Californian about it, I'm sure it's nothing but a burden.'

'No need to be so English,' said Johnny. 'I *am* honoured. Any time you want to talk about it I'm available.'

Patrick felt disarmed and infinitely sad for a moment. 'Shall we head off to this wretched party?' he said.

They walked out of the dining room together, passing David Windfall and Cindy Smith.

'There was an unexpected fluctuation in the exchange rate,' David was explaining. 'Everyone panicked like mad, except for me, the reason being that I was having a tremendously boozy lunch with Sonny in his club. At the end of the day I'd made a huge amount of money from doing absolutely nothing while everybody else had been very badly stung. My boss was absolutely livid.'

'Do you get on well with your boss?' asked Cindy who really couldn't have cared less.

'Of course I do,' said David. 'You Americans call it "internal networking", we just call it good manners.'

'Gee,' said Cindy.

'We'd better go in separate cars,' said Patrick, as he walked through the bar with Johnny, 'I might want to leave early.'

'Right,' said Johnny, 'see you there.'

8

Sonny's inner circle, the forty guests who were dining at Cheatley before the party, hung about in the Yellow Room, unable to sit down before Princess Margaret chose to.

'Do you believe in God, Nicholas?' asked Bridget, introducing Nicholas Pratt into the conversation she was having with Princess Margaret.

Nicholas rolled his eyeballs wearily, as if someone had tried to revive a tired old piece of scandal.

'What intrigues me, my dear, is whether he still believes in *us*. Or have we given the supreme schoolmaster a nervous breakdown? In any case, I think it was one of the Bibescos who said, "To a man of the world, the universe is a suburb."'

'I don't like the sound of your friend Bibesco,' said

Princess Margaret, wrinkling her nose. 'How can the universe be a suburb? It's too silly.'

'What I think he meant, ma'am,' replied Nicholas, 'is that sometimes the largest questions are the most trivial, because they cannot be answered, while the seemingly trivial ones, like where one sits at dinner,' he gave this example while raising his eyebrows at Bridget, 'are the most fascinating.'

'Aren't people funny? I don't find where one sits at dinner fascinating at all,' lied the Princess. 'Besides, as you know,' she went on, 'my sister is the head of the Church of England, and I don't like listening to atheistic views. People think they're being so clever, but it just shows a lack of humility.' Silencing Nicholas and Bridget with her disapproval, the Princess took a gulp from her glass of whisky. 'Apparently it's on the increase,' she said enigmatically.

'What is, ma'am?' asked Nicholas.

'Child abuse,' said the Princess. 'I was at a concert for the NSPCC last weekend, and they told me it's on the increase.'

'Perhaps it's just that people are more inclined to wash their dirty linen in public nowadays,' said Nicholas. 'Frankly I find *that* tendency much more worrying than all this fuss about child abuse. Children probably didn't realize they were being abused until they had to watch it on television every night. I believe in America they've started suing their parents for bringing them up badly.'

'Really?' giggled the Princess. 'I must tell Mummy, she'll be fascinated.'

Nicholas burst out laughing. 'But seriously, ma'am, the thing that worries me isn't all this child abuse, but the appalling way that people spoil their children these days.'

'Isn't it dreadful?' gasped the Princess. 'I see more and more children with absolutely no discipline at all. It's frightening.'

'Terrifying,' Nicholas confirmed.

'But I don't think that the NSPCC were talking about *our* world,' said the Princess, generously extending to Nicholas the circle of light that radiated from her presence. 'What it really shows is the emptiness of the socialist dream. They thought that every problem could be solved by throwing money at it, but it simply isn't true. People may have been poor, but they were happy because they lived in real communities. My mother says that when she visited the East End during the Blitz she met more people there with real dignity than you could hope to find in the entire corps diplomatique.'

'What I find with beautiful women,' said Peter Porlock to Robin Parker as they drifted towards the dining room, 'is that, after one's waited around for ages, they all arrive at once, as buses are supposed to do. Not that I've ever waited around for a bus, except at that British Heritage thing in Washington. Do you remember?'

'Yes, of course,' said Robin Parker, his eyes swimming in and out of focus, like pale blue goldfish, behind the thick lenses of his glasses. 'They hired a double-decker London bus for us.'

'Some people said "coals to Newcastle",' said Peter, 'but I was jolly pleased to see what I'd been missing all these years.'

Tony Fowles was full of amusing and frivolous ideas. Just as there were boxes at the opera where you could hear the music but not see the action, he said that there should be soundproof boxes where you could neither hear the music nor see the action, but just look at the other people with very powerful binoculars.

The Princess laughed merrily. Something about

Tony's effete silliness made her feel relaxed, but all too soon she was separated from him and placed next to Sonny at the far end of the table.

'Ideally, the number of guests at a private dinner party,' said Jacques d'Alantour, raising a judicious index finger, 'should be more than the graces and less than the muses! But this,' he said, spreading his hands out and closing his eyes as if words were about to fail him, 'this is something absolutely extraordinary.'

Few people were more used than the ambassador to looking at a dinner table set for forty, but Bridget smiled radiantly at him, while trying to remember how many muses there were supposed to be.

'Do you have any politics?' Princess Margaret asked Sonny.

'Conservative, ma'am,' said Sonny proudly.

'So I assumed. But are you *involved* in politics? For myself I don't mind who's in government so long as they're good at governing. What we must avoid at all costs is these windscreen wipers: left, right, left, right.'

Sonny laughed immoderately at the thought of political windscreen wipers.

'I'm afraid I'm only involved at a very local level, ma'am,' he replied. 'The Little Soddington bypass, that sort of thing. Trying to make sure that footpaths don't spring up all over the place. People seem to think that the countryside is just an enormous park for factory workers to drop their sweet papers in. Well, those of us who live here feel rather differently about it.'

'One needs someone responsible keeping an eye on things at a local level,' said Princess Margaret reassuringly. 'So many of the things that get ruined are little out-of-the-way places that one only notices once they've already been ruined. One drives past thinking how nice they must have once been.'

'You're absolutely right, ma'am,' agreed Sonny.

'Is it venison?' asked the Princess. 'It's hard to tell under this murky sauce.'

'Yes, it is venison,' said Sonny nervously. 'I'm awfully sorry about the sauce. As you say, it's perfectly disgusting.' He could remember checking with her private secretary that the Princess liked venison.

She pushed her plate away and picked up her cigarette lighter. 'I get sent fallow deer from Richmond Park,' she said smugly. 'You have to be on the list.

The Queen said to me, "Put yourself on the list," so I did.'

'How very sensible, ma'am,' simpered Sonny.

'Venison is the one meat I rr-eally don't like,' Jacques d'Alantour admitted to Caroline Porlock, 'but I don't want to create a diplomatic incident, and so . . .' He popped a piece of meat into his mouth, wearing a theatrically martyred expression which Caroline later described as being 'a bit much'.

'Do you like it? It's venison,' said Princess Margaret leaning over slightly towards Monsieur d'Alantour, who was sitting on her right.

'Really, it is something absolutely marvellous, ma'am,' said the ambassador. 'I did not know one could find such cooking in your country. The sauce is extremely subtle.' He narrowed his eyes to give an impression of subtlety.

The Princess allowed her views about the sauce to be eclipsed by the gratification of hearing England described as 'your country', which she took to be an acknowledgement of her own feeling that it belonged, if not legally, then in some much more profound sense, to her own family.

In his anxiety to show his love for the venison of

merry old England, the ambassador raised his fork with such an extravagant gesture of appreciation that he flicked glistening brown globules over the front of the Princess's blue tulle dress.

'I am prostrated with horr-rror!' he exclaimed, feeling that he was on the verge of a diplomatic incident.

The Princess compressed her lips and turned down the corners of her mouth, but said nothing. Putting down the cigarette holder into which she had been screwing a cigarette, she pinched her napkin between her fingers and handed it over to Monsieur d'Alantour.

'Wipe!' she said with terrifying simplicity.

The ambassador pushed back his chair and sank to his knees obediently, first dipping the corner of the napkin in a glass of water. While he rubbed at the spots of sauce on her dress, the Princess lit her cigarette and turned to Sonny.

'I thought I couldn't dislike the sauce more when it was on my plate,' she said archly.

'The sauce has been a disaster,' said Sonny, whose face was now maroon with extra blood. 'I can't apologize enough, ma'am.'

'There's no need for *you* to apologize,' she said.

Jacqueline d'Alantour, fearing that her husband

might be performing an act inconsistent with the dignity of France, had risen and walked around the table. Half the guests were pretending not to have noticed what was going on and the other half were not bothering to pretend.

'What I admire about P.M.,' said Nicholas Pratt, who sat on Bridget's left at the other end of the table, 'is the way she puts everyone at their ease.'

George Watford, who sat on Bridget's other side, decided to ignore Pratt's interruption and to carry on trying to explain to his hostess the purpose of the Commonwealth.

'I'm afraid the Commonwealth is completely ineffectual,' he said sadly. 'We have nothing in common, except our poverty. Still, it gives the Queen some pleasure,' he added, glancing down the table at Princess Margaret, 'and that is reason enough to keep it.'

Jacqueline, still unclear about what had happened, was amazed to find that her husband had sunk even deeper under the table and was rubbing furiously at the Princess's dress.

'*Mais tu es complètement cinglé*,' hissed Jacqueline. The sweating ambassador, like a groom in the Augean stables, had no time to look up.

'I have done something unpardonable!' he declared. 'I have splashed this wonder-fool sauce on Her Royal Highness's dress.'

'Ah, ma'am,' said Jacqueline to the Princess, girl to girl, 'he's so clumsy! Let me help you.'

'I'm quite happy to have your husband do it,' said the Princess. 'He spilled it, he should wipe it up! In fact, one feels he might have had a great career in dry cleaning if he hadn't been blown off course,' she said nastily.

'You must allow us to give you a new dress, ma'am,' purred Jacqueline, who could feel claws sprouting from her fingertips. '*Allez*, Jacques, it's enough!' She laughed.

'There's still a spot here,' said Princess Margaret bossily, pointing to a small stain on the upper edge of her lap.

The ambassador hesitated.

'Go on, wipe it up!'

Jacques dipped the corner of the napkin back into his glass of water, and attacked the spot with rapid little strokes.

'*Ah, non, mais c'est vraiment insupportable*,' snapped Jacqueline.

'What is "*insupportable*",' said the Princess in a

nasal French accent, 'is to be showered in this revolting sauce. I needn't remind you that your husband is Ambassador to the Court of St James's,' she said as if this were somehow equivalent to being her personal maid.

Jacqueline bobbed briefly and walked back to her place, but only to grab her bag and stride out of the room.

By this time the table had fallen silent.

'Oh, a silence,' declared Princess Margaret. 'I don't approve of silences. If Noël were here,' she said, turning to Sonny, 'he'd have us all in stitches.'

'Nole, ma'am?' asked Sonny, too paralysed with terror to think clearly.

'Coward, you silly,' replied the Princess. 'He could make one laugh for hours on end. It's the people who could make one laugh,' she said, puffing sensitively on her cigarette, 'whom one really misses.'

Sonny, already mortified by the presence of venison at his table, was now exasperated by the absence of Noël. The fact that Noël was long dead did nothing to mitigate Sonny's sense of failure, and he would have sunk into speechless gloom had he not been saved by the Princess, who found herself in a thoroughly good mood after asserting her dignity and establishing in such a spectacular fashion that she was the most important person in the room.

'Remind me, Sonny,' she said chattily, 'do you have any children?'

'Yes, indeed, ma'am, I have a daughter.'

'How old is she?' asked the Princess brightly.

'It's hard to believe,' said Sonny, 'but she must be seven by now. It won't be long before she's at the blue-jean stage,' he added ominously.

'Oh,' groaned the Princess, making a disagreeable face, a muscular contraction that cost her little effort, 'aren't they dreadful? They're a sort of uniform. And so scratchy. I can't imagine why one would want to look like everyone else. I know I don't.'

'Absolutely, ma'am,' said Sonny.

'When my children got to that stage,' confided the Princess, 'I said, "For goodness' sake, don't get those dreadful blue jeans," and they very sensibly went out and bought themselves some green trousers.'

'Very sensible,' echoed Sonny, who was hysterically grateful that the Princess had decided to be so friendly.

Jacqueline returned after five minutes, hoping to give the impression that she had only absented herself because, as one mistress of modern manners has put it, 'certain bodily functions are best performed in private'. In fact she had paced about her bedroom furiously until she came to the reluctant conclusion that a show of levity would in the end be less humiliating than a show of indignation. Knowing also that what her husband feared most, and had spent his career nimbly avoiding, was a diplomatic incident, she hastily applied some fresh lipstick and breezed back into the dining room.

Seeing Jacqueline return, Sonny experienced a fresh wave of anxiety, but the Princess ignored her completely and started telling him one of her stories about 'the ordinary people of this country' in whom she had 'enormous faith' based on a combination of complete ignorance about their lives and complete confidence in their royalist sympathies.

'I was in a taxi once,' she began in a tone that invited Sonny to marvel at her audacity. He duly raised his eyebrows with what he hoped was a tactful combination of surprise and admiration. 'And Tony said to the driver, "Take us to the Royal Garden Hotel," which, as you know, is at the bottom of our drive. And the driver said – ' the Princess leaned forward to deliver the punch line with a rough little jerk of her head, in what might have been mistaken by a Chinaman for a Cockney accent – ' "I know where *she* lives." '

She grinned at Sonny. 'Aren't they wonderful people?' she squawked. 'Aren't they marvellous people?'

Sonny threw back his head and roared with laughter. 'What a splendid story, ma'am,' he gasped. 'What wonderful people.'

The Princess sat back in her chair well satisfied; she had charmed her host and lent a golden touch to the evening. As to the clumsy Frenchman on her other side, she wasn't going to let him off the hook so easily. After all, it was no small matter to make a mistake in the presence of the Queen's sister. The constitution itself rested on respect for the Crown, and it was her duty (oh, how she sometimes wished she could lay it all aside! How, in fact, she sometimes did, only to scold more severely those who thought she was serious), yes, it was her *duty* to maintain that respect. It was the price she had to pay for what other people foolishly regarded as her great privileges.

Next to her the ambassador appeared to be in a kind of trance, but under his dumb surface he was composing, with the fluency of an habitual dispatch writer, his report for the Quai d'Orsay. The glory of France had not been diminished by his little gaffe. Indeed, he had turned what might have been an awkward incident into a triumphant display of gallantry and wit. It was here that the ambassador paused for a while to think of something clever he might have said at the time.

While Alantour pondered, the door of the dining room opened slowly, and Belinda, barefooted, in a white nightdress, peered around the edge of the door.

'Oh, look, it's a little person who can't sleep,' boomed Nicholas.

Bridget swivelled around and saw her daughter looking pleadingly into the room.

'Who is it?' the Princess asked Sonny.

'I'm afraid it's my daughter, ma'am,' replied Sonny, glaring at Bridget.

'Still up? She should be in bed. Go on, tuck her up immediately!' she snapped.

Something about the way she had said 'tuck her up' made Sonny momentarily forget his courtly graces and feel protective towards his daughter. He tried again to catch Bridget's eye, but Belinda had already come into the room and approached her mother.

'Why are you still up, darling?' asked Bridget.

'I couldn't sleep,' said Belinda. 'I was lonely because everyone else is down here.'

'But this is a dinner for grown-ups.'

'Which one's Princess Margaret?' asked Belinda, ignoring her mother's explanation.

'Why don't you get your mother to present you to her?' suggested Nicholas suavely. 'And then you can go to bed like a good little girl.'

'OK,' said Belinda. 'Can someone read me a story?'

'Not tonight, darling,' said her mother. 'But I'll introduce you to Princess Margaret.' She got up and walked the length of the table to Princess Margaret's side. Leaning over a little, she asked if she could present her daughter.

'No, not now, I don't think it's right,' said the Princess. 'She ought to be in bed, and she'll just get overexcited.'

'You're quite right, of course,' said Sonny. 'Honestly, darling, you must scold Nanny for letting her escape.'

'I'll take her upstairs myself,' said Bridget coldly.

'Good girl,' said Sonny, extremely angry that Nanny, who after all cost one an absolute bomb, should have shown him up in front of the Princess.

'I'm very pleased to hear that you've got the Bishop of Cheltenham for us tomorrow,' said the Princess, grinning at her host, once the door was firmly closed on his wife and daughter.

'Yes,' said Sonny. 'He seemed very nice on the phone.'

'Do you mean you don't know him?' asked the Princess.

'Not as well as I'd like to,' said Sonny, reeling from the prospect of more royal disapproval.

'He's a saint,' said the Princess warmly. 'I really think he's a saint. And a wonderful scholar: I'm told he's happier speaking in Greek than in English. Isn't it marvellous?'

'I'm afraid my Greek's a bit rusty for that sort of thing,' said Sonny.

'Don't worry,' said the Princess, 'he's the most modest man in the world, he wouldn't dream of showing you up; he just gets into these Greek trances. In his mind, you see, he's still chatting away to the apostles, and it takes him a while to notice his surroundings. Isn't it fascinating?'

'Extraordinary,' murmured Sonny.

'There won't be any hymns, of course,' said the Princess.

'But we can have some if you like,' protested Sonny.

'It's Holy Communion, silly. Otherwise I'd have you all singing hymns to see which ones I liked best.

People always seem to enjoy it, it gives one something to do after dinner on Saturday.'

'We couldn't have managed that tonight in any case,' said Sonny.

'Oh, I don't know,' said the Princess, 'we might have gone off to the library in a small group.' She beamed at Sonny, conscious of the honour she was bestowing on him by this suggestion of deeper intimacy. There was no doubt about it: when she put her mind to it she could be the most charming woman in the world.

'One had such fun practising hymns with Noël,' she went on. 'He would make up new words and one would die laughing. Yes, it might have been rather cosy in the library. I do so *hate* big parties.'

9

Patrick slammed the car door and glanced up at the stars, gleaming through a break in the clouds like fresh track marks in the dark blue limbs of the night. It was a humbling experience, he thought, making one's own medical problems seem so insignificant.

An avenue of candles, planted on either side of the drive, marked the way from the car park to the wide circle of gravel in front of the house. Its grey porticoed facade was theatrically flattened by floodlights, and looked like wet cardboard, stained by the sleet that had fallen earlier in the afternoon.

In the denuded drawing room, the fireplace was loaded with crackling wood. The champagne being poured by a flushed barman surged over the sides of glasses and subsided again to a drop. As Patrick headed down the hooped canvas tunnel that led to the tent, he heard the swell of voices rising, and sometimes laughter, like the top of a wave caught by the wind, splashing over the whole room. A room, he decided, full of uncertain fools, waiting for an amorous complication or a practical joke to release them from their awkward wanderings. Walking into the tent, he saw George Watford sitting on a chair immediately to the right of the entrance.

'George!'

'My dear, what a nice surprise,' said George, wincing as he clambered to his feet. 'I'm sitting here because I can't hear anything these days when there's a lot of noise about.'

'I thought people were supposed to lead lives of *quiet* desperation,' Patrick shouted.

'Not quiet enough,' George shouted back with a wan smile.

'Oh, look there's Nicholas Pratt,' said Patrick, sitting down next to George.

'So it is,' said George. 'With him one has to take the smooth with the smooth. I must say I never really shared your father's enthusiasm for him. I miss your father, you know, Patrick. He was a very brilliant man, but never happy, I think.'

'I hardly ever think of him these days,' said Patrick.

'Have you found something you enjoy doing?' asked George.

'Yes, but nothing one could make a career out of,' said Patrick.

'One really has to try to make a contribution,' said George. 'I can look back with reasonable satisfaction on one or two pieces of legislation that I helped steer through the House of Lords. I've also helped to keep Richfield going for the next generation. Those are the sorts of things one is left hanging on to when all the fun and games have slipped away. No man is an island – although one's known a surprising number who own one. Really a surprising number, and not just in Scotland. But one really must try to make a contribution.'

'Of course you're right,' sighed Patrick. He was rather intimidated by George's sincerity. It reminded him of the disconcerting occasion when his father had clasped his arm, and said to him, apparently without any hostile intention, 'If you have a talent, use it. Or you'll be miserable all your life.'

'Oh, look, it's Tom Charles, over there taking a drink from the waiter. He has a jolly nice island in Maine. Tom!' George called out. 'I wonder if he's spotted us. He was head of the IMF at one time, made the best of a frightfully hard job.'

'I met him in New York,' said Patrick. 'You introduced us at that club we went to after my father died.'

'Oh, yes. We all rather wondered what had happened to you,' said George. 'You left us in the lurch with that frightful bore Ballantine Morgan.'

'I was overwhelmed with emotion,' said Patrick.

'I should think it was dread at having to listen to another of Ballantine's stories. His son is here tonight. I'm afraid he's a chip off the old block, as they say. Tom!' George called out again.

Tom Charles looked around, uncertain whether he'd heard his name being called. George waved at him again. Tom spotted them, and the three men greeted each other. Patrick recognized Tom's bloodhound features. He had one of those faces that ages prematurely but then goes on looking the same forever. He might even look young in another twenty years.

'I heard about your dinner,' said Tom. 'It sounds like quite something.'

'Yes,' said George. 'I think it demonstrates again that the junior members of the royal family should pull their socks up and we should all be praying for the Queen during these difficult times.'

Patrick realized he was not joking.

'How was your dinner at Harold's?' asked George. 'Harold Greene was born in Germany,' he went on to explain to Patrick. 'As a boy he wanted to join the Hitler Youth – smashing windows and wearing all those thrilling uniforms: it's any boy's dream – but his father told him he couldn't because he was Jewish. Harold never got over the disappointment, and he's really an anti-Semite with a veneer of Zionism.'

'Oh, I don't think that's fair,' said Tom.

'Well, I don't suppose it is,' said George, 'but what is the point of reaching this idiotically advanced age if one can't be unfair?'

'There was a lot of talk at dinner about Chancellor Kohl's claim that he was "very shocked" when war broke out in the Gulf.'

'I suppose it was shocking for the poor Germans not to have started the war themselves,' George interjected.

'Harold was saying over dinner,' continued Tom, 'that he's surprised there isn't a United Nations Organisation called UNUC because "when it comes down to it they're no bloody use at all".'

'What I want to know,' said George, thrusting out his chin, 'is what chance we have against the Japanese when we live in a country where "industrial action" means going on strike. I'm afraid I've lived for too long. I can still remember when this country counted for something. I was just saying to Patrick,' he added, politely drawing him back into the conversation, 'that one has to make a contribution in life. There are too many people in this room who are just hanging around waiting for their relations to die so that they can go on more expensive holidays. Sadly, I count my daughter-in-law among them.'

'Bunch of vultures,' growled Tom. 'They'd better take those holidays soon. I don't see the banking system holding up, except on some kind of religious basis.'

'Currency always rested on blind faith,' said George.

'But it's never been like this before,' said Tom. 'Never has so much been owed by so many to so few.'

'I'm too old to care anymore,' said George. 'Do you know, I was thinking that if I go to heaven, and I don't see why I shouldn't, I hope that King, my old butler, will be there.'

'To do your unpacking?' suggested Patrick.

'Oh, no,' said George. 'I think he's done quite enough of that sort of thing down here. In any case, I don't think one takes any luggage to heaven, do you? It must be like a perfect weekend, with no luggage.'

Like a rock in the middle of a harbour, Sonny stood stoutly near the entrance of the tent putting his guests under an obligation to greet him as they came in.

'But this is something absolutely marvellous,' said Jacques d'Alantour in a confidential tone, spreading his hands to encompass the whole tent. As if responding to this gesture the big jazz band at the far end of the room struck up simultaneously.

'Well, we try our best,' said Sonny smugly.

'I think it was Henry James,' said the ambassador, who knew perfectly well that it was and had rehearsed the quotation, unearthed for him by his secretary, many times before leaving Paris, 'who said: "this richly complex English world, where the present is always seen, as it were in profile, and the past presents a full face."'

'It's no use quoting these French authors to me,' said Sonny. 'All goes over my head. But, yes, English life is rich and complex – although not as rich as it used to be with all these taxes gnawing away at the very fabric of one's house.'

'Ah,' sighed Monsieur d'Alantour sympathetically. 'But you are putting on a "brave face" tonight.'

'We've had our tricky moments,' Sonny confessed. 'Bridget went through a mad phase of thinking we knew nobody, and invited all sorts of odds and sods. Take that little Indian chap over there, for instance. He's writing a biography of Jonathan Croyden. I'd never set eyes on him before he came down to look at some letters Croyden wrote to my father, and blow me down, Bridget asked him to the party over lunch. I'm afraid I lost my temper with her afterwards, but it really was a bit much.'

'Hello, my dear,' said Nicholas to Ali Montague. 'How was your dinner?'

'Very *county*,' said Ali.

'Oh, dear. Well, ours was really *tous ce qu'il y a de plus chic*, except that Princess Margaret rapped me over the knuckles for expressing "atheistic views".'

'Even I might have a religious conversion under those circumstances,' said Ali, 'but it would be so hypocritical I'd be sent straight to hell.'

'One thing I am sure of is that if God didn't exist,

nobody would notice the difference,' said Nicholas suavely.

'Oh, I thought of you a moment ago,' said Ali. 'I overheard a couple of old men who both looked as if they'd had several riding accidents. One of them said, "I'm thinking of writing a book," and the other one replied, "Jolly good idea." "They say everyone has a book in them," said the would-be author. "Hmm, perhaps I'll write one as well," his friend replied. "Now you're stealing my idea," said the first one, really quite angrily. So naturally I wondered how your book was getting along. I suppose it must be almost finished by now.'

'It's very difficult to finish an autobiography when you're leading as thrilling a life as I am,' said Nicholas sarcastically. 'One constantly finds some new nugget that has to be put in, like a sample of your conversation, my dear.'

'There's always an element of cooperation in incest,' said Kitty Harrow knowingly. 'I know it's supposed to be fearfully taboo, but of course it's always gone on, sometimes in the very best families,' she added complacently, touching the cliff of blue-grey hair that towered over her small forehead. 'I remember my own father standing outside my bedroom door hissing, "You're completely hopeless, you've got no sexual imagination."'

'Good God!' said Robin Parker.

'My father was a marvellous man, very magnetic.' Kitty rolled her shoulders as she said this. 'Everybody adored him. So, you see, I *know* what I'm talking about. Children give off the most enormous sexual feeling; they set out to seduce their parents. It's all in Freud, I'm told, although I haven't read his books myself. I remember my son always showing me his little erection. I don't think parents should take advantage of these situations, but I can quite see how they get swept along, especially in crowded conditions with everybody living on top of each other.'

'Is your son here?' asked Robin Parker.

'No, he's in Australia,' Kitty replied sadly. 'I begged him to take over running the farm here, but he's mad about Australian sheep. I've been to see him twice, but I really can't manage the plane flight. And when I get there I'm not at all keen on that way of life, standing in a cloud of barbecue smoke being bored to death by a sheepshearer's wife – one doesn't even get the sheepshearer. Fergus took me to the coast and *forced* me to go snorkelling. All I can say is that the Great

Barrier Reef is the most vulgar thing I've ever seen. It's one's worst nightmare, full of frightful loud colours, peacock blues, and impossible oranges all higgledy-piggledy while one's mask floods.'

'The Queen was saying only the other day that London property prices are so high that she doesn't know how she'd cope without Buckingham Palace,' Princess Margaret explained to a sympathetic Peter Porlock.

'How are you?' Nicholas asked Patrick.

'Dying for a drink,' said Patrick.

'Well you have all my sympathy,' yawned Nicholas. 'I've never been addicted to heroin, but I had to give up smoking cigarettes, which was quite bad enough for me. Oh, look, there's Princess Margaret. One has to be so careful not to trip over her. I suppose you've already heard what happened at dinner.'

'The diplomatic incident.'

'Yes.'

'Very shocking,' said Patrick solemnly.

'I must say, I rather admire P.M.,' said Nicholas, glancing over at her condescendingly. 'She used a minor accident to screw the maximum amount of humiliation out of the ambassador. Somebody has to uphold our national pride during its Alzheimer years, and there's no one who does it with more conviction. Mind you,' said Nicholas in a more withering tone, '*entre nous*, since I'm relying on them to give me a lift back to London, I don't think France has been so heroically represented since the Vichy government. You should have seen the way Alantour slid to his knees. Although I'm absolutely devoted to his wife who, behind all that phoney chic, is a genuinely malicious person with whom one can have the greatest fun, I've always thought Jacques was a bit of a fool.'

'You can tell him yourself,' said Patrick as he saw the ambassador approaching from behind.

'*Mon cher* Jacques,' said Nicholas, spinning lightly round, 'I thought you were absolutely brilliant! The way you handled that tiresome woman was faultless: by giving in to her ridiculous demands you showed just how ridiculous they were. Do you know my young friend Patrick Melrose? His father was a very good friend of mine.'

'René Bollinger was such heaven,' sighed the Princess. 'He was a really great ambassador, we all absolutely adored him. It makes it all the harder to put up with the mediocrity of these two,' she added, waving her cigarette holder towards the Alantours, to whom Patrick was saying goodbye.

'I hope we didn't dr-rive away your young friend,' said Jacqueline. 'He seemed very nervous.'

'We can do without him even if I am a great advocate of diversity,' said Nicholas.

'You?' laughed Jacqueline.

'Absolutely, my dear,' Nicholas replied. 'I firmly believe that one should have the widest possible range of acquaintances, from monarchs right down to the humblest baronet in the land. With, of course, a sprinkling of superstars,' he added, like a great chef introducing a rare but pungent spice into his stew, 'before they turn, as they inevitably do, into black holes.'

'*Mais il est vraiment* too much,' said Jacqueline, delighted by Nicholas's performance.

'One's better off with a title than a mere name,' Nicholas continued. 'Proust, as I'm sure you're aware, writes very beautifully on this subject, saying that even the most fashionable commoner is bound to be forgotten very quickly, whereas the bearer of a great title is certain of immortality, at least in the eyes of his descendants.'

'Still,' said Jacqueline a little limply, 'there have been some very amusing people without titles.'

'My dear,' said Nicholas, clasping her forearm, 'what would we do without them?'

They laughed the innocent laughter of two snobs taking a holiday from that need to appear tolerant and open-minded which marred what Nicholas still called 'modern life', although he had never known any other kind.

'I feel the royal presence bearing down on us,' said Jacques uncomfortably. 'I think the diplomatic course is to explore the depths of the party.'

'My dear fellow, you are the depths of the party,' said Nicholas. 'But I quite agree, you shouldn't expose yourself to any more petulance from that absurd woman.'

'*Au revoir*,' whispered Jacqueline.

'*A bientôt*,' said Jacques, and the Alantours withdrew and separated, taking the burden of their glamour to different parts of the room.

Nicholas had hardly recovered from the loss of the Alantours when Princess Margaret and Kitty Harrow came over to his side.

'Consorting with the enemy,' scowled the Princess.

'They came to me for sympathy, ma'am,' said Nicholas indignantly, 'but I told them they'd come to the wrong place. I pointed out to him that he was a clumsy fool. And as to his absurd wife, I said that we'd had quite enough of her petulance for one evening.'

'Oh, did you?' said the Princess, smiling graciously.

'Good for you,' chipped in Kitty.

'As you saw,' boasted Nicholas, 'they slunk off with their tails between their legs. "I'd better keep a low profile," the ambassador said to me. "You've got a low enough profile already," I replied.'

'Oh, how marvellous,' said the Princess. 'Putting your sharp tongue to good use, I approve of that.'

'I suppose this'll go straight into your book,' said Kitty. 'We're all terrified, ma'am, by what Nicholas is going to say about us in his book.'

'Am I in it?' asked the Princess.

'I wouldn't dream of putting you in, ma'am,' protested Nicholas. 'I'm far too discreet.'

'You're allowed to put me in it as long as you say something nice,' said the Princess.

'I remember you when you were five years old,' said Bridget. 'You were so sweet, but rather standoffish.'

'I can't imagine why,' said Patrick. 'I remember seeing you kneeling down on the terrace just after you arrived. I was watching from behind the trees.'

'Oh God,' squealed Bridget. 'I'd forgotten that.'

'I couldn't work out what you were doing.'

'It was very shocking.'

'I'm unshockable,' said Patrick.

'Well, if you really want to know, Nicholas had told me it was something your parents did: your father making your mother eat figs off the ground, and I was rather naughtily acting out what he'd told me. He got frightfully angry with me.'

'It's nice to think of my parents having fun,' said Patrick.

'I think it was a power thing,' said Bridget, who seldom dabbled in deep psychology.

'Sounds plausible,' said Patrick.

'Oh God, there's Mummy, looking terribly lost,' said Bridget. 'You wouldn't be an angel and talk to her for a second, would you?'

'Of course,' said Patrick.

Bridget left Patrick with Virginia, congratulating herself on solving her mother problem so neatly.

'So how was your dinner here?' said Patrick, trying to open the conversation on safe ground. 'I gather

Princess Margaret got showered in brown sauce. It must have been a thrilling moment.'

'I wouldn't have found it thrilling,' said Virginia. 'I know how upsetting it can be getting a stain on your dress.'

'So you didn't actually see it,' said Patrick.

'No, I was having dinner with the Bossington-Lanes,' said Virginia.

'Really? I was supposed to be there. How was it?'

'We got lost on the way there,' sighed Virginia. 'All the cars were busy collecting people from the station, so I had to go by taxi. We stopped at a cottage that turned out to be just at the bottom of their drive and asked the way. When I said to Mr Bossington-Lane, "We had to ask the way from your neighbour in the cottage with the blue windows," he said to me, "That's not a neighbour, that's a tenant, and what's more he's a sitting tenant and a damned nuisance."'

'Neighbours are people you can ask to dinner,' said Patrick.

'That makes me his neighbour, then,' laughed Virginia. 'And I live in Kent. I don't know why my daughter told me they needed spare ladies, there were nothing but spare ladies. Mrs Bossington-Lane told me just now that she's had apologies from all four gentlemen who didn't turn up, and they all said they'd broken down on the motorway. She was very put out, after all the trouble she'd been to, but I said, "You've got to keep your sense of humour."'

'I thought she looked unconvinced when I told her I'd broken down on the motorway,' said Patrick.

'Oh,' said Virginia, clapping her hand over her mouth. 'You must have been one of them. I'd forgotten you said you were supposed to have dinner there.'

'Don't worry,' smiled Patrick. 'I just wish we'd compared stories before all telling her the same one.'

Virginia laughed. 'You've got to keep your sense of humour,' she repeated.

'What is it, darling?' asked Aurora Donne. 'You look as if you've seen a ghost.'

'Oh, I don't know,' sighed Bridget. 'I just saw Cindy Smith with Sonny – and I remember saying that we couldn't ask her because we didn't know her, and thinking it was odd of Sonny to make a thing of it – and now she's here and there was something familiar about the way they stood together, but I'm probably just being paranoid.'

Aurora, presented with the choice of telling a friend

a painful truth which could do her no possible good, or reassuring her, felt no hesitation in taking the first course for the sake of 'honesty', and the pleasure of seeing Bridget's enjoyment of her expensive life, which Aurora had often told herself she would have handled better, spoiled.

'I don't know whether I should tell you this,' said Aurora. 'I probably shouldn't.' She frowned, glancing at Bridget.

'What?' Bridget implored her. 'You've got to tell me.'

'No,' said Aurora. 'It'll only upset you. It was stupid of me to mention it.'

'You *have* to tell me now,' said Bridget desperately.

'Well, of course you're the last to know – one always is in these situations, but it's been fairly common knowledge . . .' Aurora lingered suggestively on the word 'common' which she had always been fond of, 'that Sonny and Miss Smith have been having an affair for some time.'

'God,' said Bridget. 'So that's who it is. I knew something was going on . . .' She suddenly felt very tired and sad, and looked as if she was going to cry.

'Oh, darling, don't,' said Aurora. 'Chin up,' she added consolingly.

But Bridget was overwhelmed and went up with Aurora to her bedroom and told her all about the telephone call she'd overheard that morning, swearing her to a secrecy to which Aurora swore several other people before the evening was out. Bridget's friend advised her to 'go on the warpath', thinking this was the policy likely to yield the largest number of amusing anecdotes.

'Oh, do come and help us,' said China who was sitting with Angus Broghlie and Amanda Pratt. It was not a group that Patrick had any appetite to join.

'We're making a list of all the people whose fathers aren't really their fathers,' she explained.

'Hmm, I'd do anything to be on it,' groaned Patrick. 'Anyway, it would take far too long to do in one evening.'

David Windfall, driven by a fanatical desire to exonerate himself from the blame of bringing Cindy Smith and making his hostess angry, rushed up to his fellow guests to explain that he had just been obeying orders, and it wasn't really his idea. He was about to make the same speech to Peter Porlock when he realized that Peter, as Sonny's best friend, might view it as faint-hearted, and so he checked himself and remarked instead on 'that dreadful christening' where they had last met.

'Dreadful,' confirmed Peter. 'What's the vestry for, if it isn't to dump babies along with one's umbrella and so forth? But of course the vicar wanted all the children in the church. He's a sort of flower child who believes in swinging services, but the purpose of the Church of England is to be the Church of England. It's a force of social cohesion. If it's going to get evangelical we don't want anything to do with it.'

'Hear, hear,' said David. 'I gather Bridget's very upset about my bringing Cindy Smith,' he added, unable to keep away from the subject.

'Absolutely furious,' laughed Peter. 'She had a blazing row with Sonny in the library, I'm told: audible above the band and the din, apparently. Poor Sonny, he's been locked in there all evening,' grinned Peter, nodding his head towards the door. 'Stole in there to have a *tête-à-tête*, or rather a *jambe-à-jambe*, I should imagine, with Miss Smith, then the blazing row, and now he's stuck with Robin Parker trying to cheer himself up by having his Poussin authenticated. The thing is for you to stick to your story. You met Cindy, wife couldn't come, asked her instead, foolishly didn't check, nothing to do with Sonny. Something along those lines.'

'Of course,' said David who had already told a dozen people the opposite story.

'Bridget didn't actually see them at it, and you know how women are in these situations: they believe what they want to believe.'

'Hmm,' said David, who'd already told Bridget he was just obeying orders. He winced as he saw Sonny emerging from the library nearby. Did Sonny know that he'd told Bridget?

'Sonny!' squealed David, his voice slipping into falsetto.

Sonny ignored him and boomed, 'It is a Poussin!' to Peter.

'Oh, well done,' said Peter, as if Sonny had painted it himself. 'Best possible birthday present to find that it's the real thing and not just a "school of"—'

'The trees,' said Robin, slipping his hand inside his dinner jacket for a moment, 'are unmistakable.'

'Will you excuse us?' Sonny asked Robin, still ignoring David. 'I have to have a word with Peter in private.' Sonny and Peter went into the library and closed the door.

'I've been a bloody fool,' said Sonny. 'Not least for

trusting David Windfall. That's the last time I'm having him under my roof. And now I've got a wife crisis on my hands.'

'Don't be too hard on yourself,' said Peter needlessly.

'Well, you know, I was driven to it,' said Sonny, immediately taking up Peter's suggestion. 'I mean, Bridget's not having a son and everything has been frightfully hard. But when it comes to the crunch I'm not sure I'd like life here without the old girl running the place. Cindy has got some very peculiar ideas. I'm not sure what they are, but I can sense it.'

'The trouble is it's all become so complicated,' said Peter. 'One doesn't really know where one stands with women. I mean, I was reading about this sixteenth-century Russian marriage-guidance thing, and it advises you to beat your wife lovingly so as not to render her permanently blind or deaf. If you said that sort of thing nowadays they'd string you up. But, you know, there's a lot in it, obviously in a slightly milder form. It's like the old adage about native bearers: "Beat them for no reason and they won't give you a reason to beat them."'

Sonny looked a little bewildered. As he later told some of his friends, 'When it was all hands on deck with the Bridget crisis, I'm afraid Peter didn't really pull his weight. He just waffled on about sixteenth-century Russian pamphlets.'

'It was that lovely judge Melford Stevens,' said Kitty, 'who said to a rapist, "I shall not send you to prison but back to the Midlands, which is punishment enough." I know one isn't meant to say that sort of thing, but it is rather marvellous, isn't it? I mean England used to be full of that sort of wonderfully eccentric character, but now everybody is so grey and goody-goody.'

'I frightfully dislike this bit,' said Sonny, struggling to keep up the appearance of a jovial host. 'Why does the band leader introduce the musicians, as if anyone wanted to know their names? I mean, one's given up announcing one's own guests, so why should these chaps get themselves announced?'

'Couldn't agree with you more, old bean,' said Alexander Politsky. 'In Russia, the grand families had their own estate band, and there was no more question of introducing them than there was of presenting your scullion to a grand duke. When we went shooting and there was a cold river to cross, the beaters would lie in the water and form a sort of bridge. Nobody felt they had to know their names in order to walk over their heads.'

'I think that's going a bit far,' said Sonny. 'I mean, walking over their heads. But, you see, that's why we didn't have a revolution.'

'The reason you didn't have a revolution, old bean,' said Alexander, 'is because you had two of them: the Civil War and the Glorious one.'

'And on cornet,' said Joe Martin, the band leader, '"Chilly Willy" Watson!'

Patrick, who had been paying almost no attention to the introductions, was intrigued by the sound of a familiar name. It certainly couldn't be the Chilly Willy he'd known in New York. He must be dead by now. Patrick glanced round anyway to have a look at the man who was standing up in the front row to play his brief solo. With his bulging cheeks and his dinner jacket he couldn't have been less reminiscent of the street junkie whom Patrick had scored from in Alphabet City. Chilly Willy had been a toothless, hollow-cheeked scavenger, shuffling about on the edge of oblivion, clutching on to a pair of trousers too baggy for his cadaverous frame. This jazz musician was vigorous and talented, and definitely black, whereas Chilly, with his jaundice and his pallor, although obviously a black man, had managed to look yellow.

Patrick moved towards the edge of the bandstand to have a closer look. There were probably thousands of Chilly Willys and it was absurd to think that this one was 'his'. Chilly had sat down again after playing his solo and Patrick stood in front of him frowning curiously, like a child at the zoo, feeling that talking was a barrier he couldn't cross.

'Hi,' said Chilly Willy, over the sound of a trumpet solo.

'Nice solo,' said Patrick.

'Thanks.'

'You're not . . . I knew someone in New York called Chilly Willy!'

'Where'd he live?'

'Eighth Street.'

'Uh-huh,' said Chilly. 'What did he do?'

'Well, he . . . sold . . . he lived on the streets really . . . that's why I knew it couldn't be you. Anyway, he was older.'

'I remember you!' laughed Chilly. 'You're the English guy with the coat, right?'

'That's right!' said Patrick. 'It is you! Christ, you look well. I practically didn't recognize you. You play really well too.'

'Thanks. I was always a musician, then I . . .' Chilly made a diving motion with his hand, glancing sideways at his fellow musicians.

'What happened to your wife?'

'She OD'd,' said Chilly sadly.

'Oh, I'm sorry,' said Patrick, remembering the horse syringe she had carefully unwrapped from the loo paper and charged him twenty dollars for. 'Well, it's a miracle you're alive,' he added.

'Yeah, everything's a miracle, man,' said Chilly. 'It's a fuckin' miracle we don't melt in the bath like a piece of soap.'

'The Herberts have always had a weakness for low life,' said Kitty Harrow. 'Look at Shakespeare.'

'They were certainly scraping the barrel with him,' said Nicholas. 'Society used to consist of a few hundred families all of whom knew each other. Now it just consists of one: the Guinnesses. I don't know why they don't make an address book with an especially enlarged G spot.'

Kitty giggled.

'Oh, well, I can see that you're an entrepreneur *manqué*,' said Ali to Nicholas.

'That dinner at the Bossington-Lanes' was beyond anything,' said Ali Montague to Laura and China. 'I knew we were in trouble when our host said, "The great thing about having daughters is that you can get them to fag for you." And when that great horsy girl of his came back she said, "You can't argue with Daddy, he used to have exactly the same vital statistics as Muhammad Ali, except he was a foot and a half shorter."'

Laura and China laughed. Ali was such a good mimic.

'The mother's absolutely terrified,' said Laura, 'because some friend of Charlotte's went up to "the Metrop" to share a flat with a couple of other county gals, and the first week she fell in with someone called "Evil John"!'

They all howled with laughter.

'What really terrifies Mr Bossington-Lane,' said Ali, 'is Charlotte getting an education.'

'Fat chance,' said Laura.

'He was complaining about a neighbour's daughter who had "a practically unheard of number of Os".'

'What, three?' suggested China.

'I think it was five and she was going on to do an A level in history of art. I asked him if there was any money in art, just to get him going.'

'And what did he say?' asked China.

Ali thrust out his chin and pushed a hand into his dinner jacket pocket with a thumb resting over the edge.

'"Money?" he boomed. "Not for most of them. But you know, one's dealing with people who are too busy struggling with the meaning of life to worry about that sort of thing. Not that one isn't struggling a bit oneself!" I said I thought the meaning of life included a large income. "And capital," he said.'

'The daughter is impossible,' grinned Laura. 'She told me a really boring story that I couldn't be bothered to listen to, and then ended it by saying, "Can you imagine anything worse than having your barbecue sausage stolen?" I said, "Yes, easily." And she made a dreadful honking sound and said, "Well, obviously, I didn't mean *literally*."'

'Still, it's nice of them to have us to stay,' said China provocatively.

'Do you know how many of those horrid porcelain knick-knacks I counted in my room?' Ali asked with a supercilious expression on his face to exaggerate the shock of the answer he was about to give.

'How many?' asked Laura.

'One hundred and thirty-seven.'

'A hundred and thirty-seven,' gasped China.

'And, apparently, if one of them moves, she knows about it,' said Ali.

'She once had everyone's luggage searched because one of the knick-knacks had been taken from the bedroom to the bathroom or the bathroom to the bedroom, and she thought it was stolen.'

'It's quite tempting to try and smuggle one out,' said Laura.

'Do you know what's rather fascinating?' said Ali, hurrying on to his next insight. 'That old woman with the nice face and the ghastly blue dress was Bridget's mother.'

'No!' said Laura. 'Why wasn't she at dinner here?'

'Embarrassed,' said Ali.

'How awful,' said China.

'Mind you, I do see what she means,' said Ali. 'The mother *is* rather Surrey Pines.'

'I saw Debbie,' said Johnny.

'Really? How was she looking?' asked Patrick.

'Beautiful.'

'She always looked beautiful at big parties,' said Patrick. 'I must talk to her one of these days. It's easy to forget that she's just another human being, with a body and a face and almost certainly a cigarette, and that she may well no longer be the same person that I knew.'

'How have you been feeling since dinner?' asked Johnny.

'Pretty weird to begin with, but I'm glad we talked.'

'Good,' said Johnny. He felt awkward not knowing what more to say about their earlier conversation, but not wanting to pretend it had never happened. 'Oh, I thought of you during my meeting,' he said with artificial brightness. 'There was this man who had to switch off his television last night because he thought he was putting the presenters off.'

'Oh, I used to get that,' said Patrick. 'When my father died in New York one of the longest conversations I had (if I is the right pronoun in this case) was with the television set.'

'I remember you telling me,' said Johnny.

The two men fell silent and stared at the throng that struggled under wastes of grey velvet with the same frantic but restricted motion as bacteria multiplying under a microscope.

'It takes about a hundred of these ghosts to precipitate one flickering and disreputable sense of identity,' said Patrick. 'These are the sort of people who were around during my childhood: hard dull people who seemed quite sophisticated but were in fact as ignorant as swans.'

'They're the last Marxists,' said Johnny unexpectedly. 'The last people who believe that class is a total explanation. Long after that doctrine has been abandoned in Moscow and Peking it will continue to flourish under the marquees of England. Although most of them have the courage of a half-eaten worm,' he continued, warming to his theme, 'and the intellectual vigour of dead sheep, they are the true heirs to Marx and Lenin.'

'You'd better go and tell them,' said Patrick. 'I think most of them were expecting to inherit a bit of Gloucestershire instead.'

'Every man has his price,' said Sonny tartly. 'Wouldn't you agree, Robin?'

'Oh, yes,' said Robin, 'but he must make sure that his price isn't too low.'

'I'm sure most people are very careful to do that,' said Sonny, wondering what would happen if Robin blackmailed him.

'But it's not just money that corrupts people,' said Jacqueline d'Alantour. 'We had the most wonder-fool driver called Albert. He was a very sweet, gentle man who used to tell the most touching story you could imagine about operating on his goldfish. One day, when Jacques was going shooting, his loader fell ill and so he said, "I'll have to take Albert." I said, "But you can't, it will kill him, he adores animals, he won't be able to bear the sight of all that blood." But Jacques insisted, and he's a very stubborn man, so there was nothing I could do. When the first few birds were shot, poor Albert was in agony,' Jacqueline covered her eyes theatrically, 'but then he started to get interested,' she parted her fingers and peeped out between them. 'And now,' she said, flinging her hands down, 'he subscribes to the *Shooting Times*, and has every kind of gun magazine you can possibly imagine. It's become quite dangerous to drive around with him because every time there's a pigeon, which in London is every two metres, he says, "Monsieur d'Alantour would get that one." When we go through Trafalgar Square, he doesn't look at the road at all, he just stares at the sky, and makes shooting noises.'

'I shouldn't think you could eat a London pigeon,' said Sonny sceptically.

'Patrick Melrose? You're not David Melrose's son, by any chance?' asked Bunny Warren, a figure Patrick could hardly remember, but a name that had floated around his childhood at a time when his parents still had a social life, before their divorce.

'Yes.'

Bunny's creased face, like an animated sultana, raced through half a dozen expressions of surprise and delight. 'I remember you as a child, you used to take a running kick at my balls each time I came to Victoria Road for a drink.'

'I'm sorry about that,' said Patrick. 'Oddly enough, Nicholas Pratt was complaining about the same sort of thing this morning.'

'Oh, well, in his case . . .' said Bunny with a mischievous laugh.

'I used to get to the right velocity,' Patrick explained, 'by starting on the landing and running down the first flight of stairs. By the time I reached the hall I could manage a really good kick.'

'You don't have to tell me,' said Bunny. 'Do you know, it's a funny thing,' he went on in a more serious tone, 'hardly a day passes without my thinking of your father.'

'Same here,' said Patrick, 'but I've got a good excuse.'

'So have I,' said Bunny. 'He helped me at a time when I was in an extremely wobbly state.'

'He helped to put me *into* an extremely wobbly state,' said Patrick.

'I know a lot of people found him difficult,' admitted Bunny, 'and he may have been at his most difficult with his children – people usually are – but I saw another side of his personality. After Lucy died, at a time when I really couldn't cope at all, he took care of me and stopped me drinking myself to death, listened with enormous intelligence to hours of black despair, and never used what I told him against me.'

'The fact that you mention his not using anything you said against you is sinister enough.'

'You can say what you like,' said Bunny bluntly, 'but your father probably saved my life.' He made an inaudible excuse and moved away abruptly.

Alone in the press of the party, Patrick was suddenly anxious to avoid another conversation, and left the tent, preoccupied by what Bunny had said about his father. As he hurried into the now-crowded drawing room, he was spotted by Laura, who stood with China and a man Patrick did not recognize.

'Hello, darling,' said Laura.

'Hi,' said Patrick, who didn't want to be waylaid.

'Have you met Ballantine Morgan?' said China.

'Hello,' said Patrick.

'Hello,' said Ballantine, giving Patrick an annoyingly firm handshake. 'I was just saying,' he continued, 'that I've been lucky enough to inherit what is probably the greatest gun collection in the world.'

'Well, I think,' said Patrick, 'I was lucky enough to see a book about it shown to me by your father.'

'Oh, so you've read *The Morgan Gun Collection*,' said Ballantine.

'Well, not from cover to cover, but enough to know how extraordinary it was to own the greatest gun collection in the world and be such a good shot, as well as write about the whole thing in such beautiful prose.'

'My father was also a very fine photographer,' said Ballantine.

'Oh, yes, I knew I'd forgotten something,' said Patrick.

'He was certainly a multitalented individual,' said Ballantine.

'When did he die?' asked Patrick.

'He died of cancer last year,' said Ballantine. 'When a man of my father's wealth dies of cancer, you know they haven't found a cure,' he added with justifiable pride.

'It does you great credit that you're such a fine curator of his memory,' said Patrick wearily.

'Honour thy father and thy mother all thy days,' said Ballantine.

'That's certainly been my policy,' Patrick affirmed.

China, who felt that even Ballantine's gargantuan income might be eclipsed by his fatuous behaviour, suggested that they dance.

'I'd be pleased to,' said Ballantine. 'Excuse us,' he added to Laura and Patrick.

'What a ghastly man,' said Laura.

'You should have met his father,' said Patrick.

'If he could get that silver spoon out of his mouth—'

'He would be even more pointless than he already is,' said Patrick.

'How are you, anyway, darling?' Laura asked. 'I'm pleased to see you. This party is really getting on my nerves. Men used to tell me how they used butter for sex, now they tell me how they've eliminated it from their diet.'

Patrick smiled. 'You certainly have to kick a lot of bodies out there before you find a live one,' he said. 'There's a blast of palpable stupidity that comes from our host, like opening the door of a sauna. The best way to contradict him is to let him speak.'

'We could go upstairs,' said Laura.

'What on earth for?' smiled Patrick.

'We could just fuck. No strings.'

'Well, it's something to do,' said Patrick.

'Thanks,' said Laura.

'No, no, I'm really keen,' said Patrick. 'Although I can't help thinking it's a terrible idea. Aren't we going to get confused?'

'No strings, remember?' said Laura, marching him towards the hall.

A security guard stood at the foot of the staircase. 'I'm sorry, no one goes upstairs,' he said.

'We're staying here,' said Laura, and something indefinably arrogant about her tone made the security man step aside.

Patrick and Laura kissed, leaning against the wall of the attic room they had found.

'Guess who I'm having an affair with?' asked Laura as she detached herself.

'I dread to think. Anyhow, why do you want to discuss it just now?' Patrick mumbled as he bit her neck.

'He's someone you know.'

'I give up,' sighed Patrick who could feel his erection dwindling.

'Johnny.'

'Well, that's put me right off,' said Patrick.

'I thought you might want to steal me back.'

'I'd rather stay friends with Johnny. I don't want more irony and more tension. You never really understood that, did you?'

'You love irony and tension, what are you talking about?'

'You just go round imagining everybody's like you.'

'Oh, fuck off,' said Laura. 'Or as Lawrence Harvey says in *Darling*, "Put away your Penguin Freud."'

'Look, we'd better just part now, don't you think?' said Patrick. 'Before we have a row.'

'God, you're a pain,' said Laura.

'Let's go down separately,' said Patrick. The flickering flame of his lighter cast a dim wobbling light over the room. The lighter went out, but Patrick found the brass doorknob and, opening the door cautiously, allowed a wedge of light to cross the dusty floorboards.

'You go first,' he whispered, brushing the dust from the back of her dress.

'Bye,' she said curtly.

10

Patrick closed the door gratefully and lit a cigarette. Since his conversation with Bunny there'd been no time to think, but now the disturbing quality of Bunny's remarks caught up with him and kept him in the attic.

Even when he had gone to New York to collect his ashes, Patrick had not been completely convinced by the simple solution of loathing his father. Bunny's loyalty to David made Patrick realize that his real difficulty might be in acknowledging the same feelings in himself.

What had there been to admire about his father? The music he had refused to take the risk of recording? And yet it had sometimes broken Patrick's heart to hear it. The psychological insight he had habitually used to torment his friends and family, but which

Bunny claimed had saved his life? All of David's virtues and talents had been double-edged, but however vile he had been he had not been deluded, most of the time, and had accepted with some stoicism his well-deserved suffering.

It was not admiration that would reconcile him to his father, or even the famously stubborn love of children for their parents, able to survive far worse fates than Patrick's. The greenish faces of those drowning figures clinging to the edge of the *Medusa*'s raft haunted his imagination, and he did not always picture them *from* the raft, but often as enviably closer to it than he was. How many choked cursing? How many slipped under silently? How many survived a little longer by pressing on the shoulders of their drowning neighbours?

Something more practical made him rummage about for a reason to make peace. Most of Patrick's strengths, or what he imagined were his strengths, derived from his struggle against his father, and only by becoming detached from their tainted origin could he make any use of them.

And yet he could never lose his indignation at the way his father had cheated him of any peace of mind, and he knew that however much trouble he put into repairing himself, like a once-broken vase that looks whole on its patterned surface but reveals in its pale interior the thin dark lines of its restoration, he could only produce an illusion of wholeness.

All Patrick's attempts at generosity ran up against his choking indignation while, on the other hand, his hatred ran up against those puzzling moments, fleeting and always spoiled, when his father had seemed to be in love with life and to take pleasure in any expression of freedom, or playfulness, or brilliance. Perhaps he would have to settle for the idea that it must have been even worse being his father than being someone his father had attempted to destroy.

Simplification was dangerous and would later take its revenge. Only when he could hold in balance his hatred and his stunted love, looking on his father with neither pity nor terror but as another human being who had not handled his personality especially well; only when he could live with the ambivalence of never forgiving his father for his crimes but allowing himself to be touched by the unhappiness that had produced them as well as the unhappiness they had produced, could he be released, perhaps, into a new life that would enable him to live instead of merely surviving. He might even enjoy himself.

Patrick grunted nervously. Enjoy himself? He mustn't let his optimism run away with him. His eyes had adjusted to the dark and he could now make out the chests and boxes that surrounded the small patch of floor he had been pacing around. A narrow half window giving onto the roof and gutter caught the murky brown glow of the floodlights at the front of the house. He lit another cigarette and smoked it, leaning against the windowsill. He felt the usual panic about needing to be elsewhere, in this case downstairs where he couldn't help imagining the carpets being hoovered and the caterers' vans loaded, although it had only been about one thirty when he came upstairs with Laura. But he stayed in the attic, intrigued by the slightest chance of release from the doldrums in which his soul had lain breathless for so long.

Patrick opened the window to throw his cigarette onto the damp roof. Taking a last gulp of smoke, he smiled at the thought that David probably would have shared his point of view about their relationship. It was the kind of trick that had made him a subtle enemy, but now it might help to end their battle. Yes, his father would have applauded Patrick's defiance and understood his efforts to escape the maze into which he had placed him. The thought that he would have wanted him to succeed made Patrick want to cry.

Beyond bitterness and despair there was something poignant, something he found harder to admit than the facts about his father's cruelty, the thing he had not been able to say to Johnny: that his father had wanted, through the brief interludes of his depression, to love him, and that he had wanted to be able to love his father, although he never would.

And why, while he was at it, continue to punish his mother? She had not done anything so much as failed to do anything, but he had put himself beyond her reach, clinging onto the adolescent bravado of pretending that she was a person he had nothing in common with at all, who just happened to have given birth to him; that their relationship was a geographical accident, like that of being someone's neighbour. She had frustrated her husband by refusing to go to bed with him, but Patrick would be the last person to blame her for that. It would probably be better if women arrested in their own childhood didn't have children with tormented misogynist homosexual paedophiles, but nothing was perfect in this sublunary world, thought Patrick, glancing up devoutly at the moon which was of course hidden, like the rest of the sky during an English winter, by a low swab of dirty cloud. His mother was really a good person, but like almost everybody she had found her compass spinning in the magnetic field of intimacy.

He really must go downstairs now. Obsessed by punctuality and dogged by a heart-compressing sense of urgency, Patrick was still incapable of keeping a watch. A watch might have soothed him by challenging his hysteria and pessimism. He would definitely get a watch on Monday. If he was not going to have an epiphany to take with him from the attic, the promise of a watch might at least represent a shimmering of hope. Wasn't there a single German word meaning 'shimmering of hope'? There was probably a single German word meaning, 'Regeneration through Punctuality, Shimmering of Hope, and Taking Pleasure in the Misfortune of Others'. If only he knew what it was.

Could one have a time-release epiphany, an epiphany without realizing it had happened? Or were they always trumpeted by angels and preceded by temporary blindness, Patrick wondered, as he walked down the corridor in the wrong direction.

Turning the corner, he saw that he was in a part of the house he had never seen before. A threadbare brown carpet stretched down a corridor that ended in darkness.

'How the fuck do you get out of this fucking house?' he cursed.

'You're going the wrong way.'

Patrick looked to his right and saw a girl in a white nightie sitting on a short flight of stairs.

'I didn't mean to swear,' he said. 'Or rather, I did mean to, but I didn't know you'd overhear me.'

'It's all right,' she said, 'Daddy swears all the time.'

'Are you Sonny and Bridget's daughter?'

'Yes. I'm Belinda.'

'Can't you get to sleep?' asked Patrick, sitting down on the stairs next to her. She shook her head. 'Why not?'

'Because of the party. Nanny said if I said my prayers properly I'd go to sleep, but I didn't.'

'Do you believe in God?' asked Patrick.

'I don't know,' said Belinda. 'But if there is a God he's not very good at it.'

Patrick laughed. 'But why aren't you at the party?' he asked.

'I'm not allowed. I'm meant to go to bed at nine.'

'How mean,' said Patrick. 'Do you want me to smuggle you down?'

'Mummy would see me. And Princess Margaret said I had to go to bed.'

'In that case we must definitely smuggle you down. Or I could read you a story.'

'Oh, that would be nice,' said Belinda, and then she put her fingers to her lips and said, 'Shh, there's someone coming.'

At that moment Bridget rounded the corner of the corridor and saw Patrick and Belinda together on the stairs.

'What are you doing here?' she asked Patrick.

'I was just trying to find my way back to the party and I ran into Belinda.'

'But what were you doing here in the first place?'

'Hello, Mummy,' interrupted Belinda.

'Hello, darling,' said Bridget, holding out her hand.

'I came up here with a girl,' Patrick explained.

'Oh God, you're making me feel very old,' said Bridget. 'So much for the security.'

'I was just going to read Belinda a story.'

'Sweet,' said Bridget. 'I should have been doing that years ago.' She picked Belinda up in her arms. 'You're so heavy, nowadays,' she groaned, smiling at Patrick firmly, but dismissively.

'Well, good night,' said Patrick, getting up from the stairs.

'Night,' yawned Belinda.

'I've got something I have to tell you,' said Bridget, as she started to carry Belinda down the corridor. 'Mummy is going to stay at Granny's tonight, and we'd like you to come along as well. There won't be any room for Nanny, though.'

'Oh good, I hate Nanny.'

'I know, darling,' said Bridget.

'But why are we going to Granny's?'

Patrick could no longer hear what they were saying as they went round the corner of the corridor.

Johnny Hall had been curious to meet Peter Porlock ever since Laura told him that Peter had needlessly paid for one of her abortions. When Laura introduced them, Peter wasted no time in swearing Johnny to secrecy about this 'dreadful Cindy and Sonny thing'.

'Of course I've known about it for ages,' he began.

'Whereas I had no idea,' David Windfall chipped in, 'even when Sonny asked me to bring her.'

'That's funny,' said Laura, 'I thought everybody knew.'

'Some people may have suspected, but nobody knew the details,' said Peter proudly.

'Not even Sonny and Cindy,' mocked Laura.

David, who was already apprised of Peter's superior knowledge, drifted off and Laura followed.

Left alone with Johnny, Peter tried to correct any impression of frivolity he might have given by saying how worried he was about his 'ailing papa' to whom he had not bothered to address a word all evening. 'Are your parentals still alive?' he asked.

'And kicking,' said Johnny. 'My mother would have managed to give an impression of mild disappointment if I'd become the youngest Prime Minister of England, so you can imagine what she feels about a moderately successful journalist. She reminds me of a story about Henry Miller visiting his dying mother with a pilot friend of his called Vincent. The old woman looked at her son and then at Vincent and said, "If only I could have a son like you, Vincent."'

'Look here, you won't leak anything I've said to the press, will you?' asked Peter.

'Alas, the editorial pages of *The Times* aren't yet given over entirely to love-nest scandals,' said Johnny contemptuously.

'Oh, *The Times*,' murmured Peter. 'Well, I know it's

frightfully unfashionable, but I still think one should practise filial loyalty. It's been frightfully easy for me: my mother was a saint and my father's the most decent chap you could hope to meet.'

Johnny smiled vaguely, wishing Laura had charged Peter double.

'Peter!' said a concerned Princess Margaret.

'Oh, ma'am, I didn't see you,' said Peter, bowing his head briefly.

'I think you should go to the hall. I'm afraid your father isn't at all well, and he's being taken off by ambulance.'

'Good God,' said Peter. 'Please excuse me, ma'am, I'll go immediately.'

The Princess, who had announced in the hall that she would tell Peter herself, and forced her lady-in-waiting to intercept other well-wishers on the same mission, was thoroughly impressed by her own goodness.

'And who are you?' she asked Johnny in the most gracious possible manner.

'Johnny Hall,' said Johnny, extending a hand.

The republican omission of ma'am, and the thrusting and unacceptable invitation to a handshake, were enough to convince the Princess that Johnny was a man of no importance.

'It must be funny having the same name as so many other people,' she speculated. 'I suppose there are hundreds of John Halls up and down the country.'

'It teaches one to look for distinction elsewhere and not to rely on an accident of birth,' said Johnny casually.

'That's where people go wrong,' said the Princess, compressing her lips, 'there is no accident in birth.'

She swept on before Johnny had a chance to reply.

Patrick walked down towards the first floor, the hubbub of the party growing louder as he descended past portraits by Lely and Lawrence and even a pair, dominating the first-floor landing, by Reynolds. The prodigious complacency which the Gravesend genes had carried from generation to generation, without the usual interludes of madness, diffidence or distinction, had defied the skills of all these painters, and, despite their celebrity, none of them had been able to make anything appealing out of the drooping eyelids and idiotically arrogant expressions of their sitters.

Thinking about Belinda, Patrick started half-consciously to walk down the stairs as he had in moments of stress when he was her age, leading with one foot and bringing the other down firmly beside it on the same step. As he approached the hall he felt an overwhelming urge to cast himself forward onto the stone floor, but stopped instead and held onto the banister, intrigued by this strange impulse, which he could not immediately explain.

Yvette had told him many times about the day he had fallen down the stairs at Lacoste and cut his hand. The story of his screams and the broken glass and Yvette's fear that he had cut a tendon had installed themselves in his picture of childhood as an accepted anecdote, but now Patrick could feel the revival of the memory itself: he could remember imagining the frames of the pictures flying down the corridor and embedding themselves in his father's chest, and decapitating Nicholas Pratt. He could feel the despairing urge to jump down the stairs to hide his guilt at snapping the stem of the glass by squeezing it so tightly. He stood on the stairs and remembered everything.

The security guard looked at him sceptically. He'd been worried ever since he allowed Patrick and Laura to go upstairs. Laura's coming down on her own and claiming that Patrick was still in their room had strengthened his suspicions. Now Patrick was behaving very eccentrically, trailing one leg as he came down the stairs, staring at the ground. He must be on drugs, thought the security guard angrily. If he had his way he'd arrest Patrick and all the other rich cunts who thought they were above the law.

Patrick, noticing the expression of hostility on the security guard's face, surfaced into the present, smiled weakly, and walked down the final steps. Across the hall, through the windows on either side of the open front door, he could see a flashing blue light.

'Are the police here?' Patrick asked.

'No, it's not the police,' said the security guard sadly. 'Ambulance.'

'What happened?'

'One of the guests had a heart attack.'

'Do you know who it was?' said Patrick.

'Don't know his name, no. White-haired gentleman.' Cold air swept into the hall through the open door. Snow was falling outside. Noticing Tom Charles standing in the doorway, Patrick went over to his side.

'It's George,' said Tom. 'I think he had a stroke. He was very weak, but he could still talk, so I hope he'll be all right.'

'So do I,' said Patrick, who had known George all

his life and suddenly realized that he would miss him if he died. George had always been friendly to him, and he urgently wanted to thank him. 'Do you know which hospital they're taking him to?'

'Cheltenham Hospital for tonight,' answered Tom. 'Sonny wants to move him to a clinic, but this ambulance is from the hospital, and I guess the priority is to keep him alive rather than to get him a more expensive room.'

'Quite,' said Patrick. 'Well, I hope King won't be unpacking for him tonight,' he added.

'Don't forget he's travelling light,' said Tom. 'Heaven is the ideal country weekend without any luggage.'

Patrick smiled. 'Let's go and see him tomorrow before lunch.'

'Good idea,' said Tom. 'Where are you staying?'

'The Little Soddington House Hotel,' said Patrick. 'Do you want me to write it down?'

'No,' said Tom, 'with a name like that I may never shake it off.'

'I think it was Talleyrand,' suggested Jacques d'Alantour, pouting a little before his favourite quotation, 'who said,' he paused, '"Doing and saying nothing are great powers, but they should not be abused."'

'Well, nobody could accuse you of doing and saying nothing this evening,' said Bridget.

'Nevertheless,' he continued, 'I shall speak to the Princess about this matter, which I hope will not become known as "*l'affaire Alantour*".' He chuckled. 'And I hope we can get the bull out of the china shop.'

'Do what you like,' said Bridget. 'I'm past caring.'

Monsieur d'Alantour, too pleased with his new plan to notice his hostess's indifference, bowed and turned on his heels.

'When the Queen's away, I become regent and head of the Privy Council,' Princess Margaret was explaining with satisfaction to Kitty Harrow.

'Ma'am,' said Monsieur d'Alantour, who after considerable thought had worked out the perfect formula for his apology.

'Oh, are you still here,' said the Princess.

'As you can see . . .' said the ambassador.

'Well, shouldn't you be setting off now? You've got a very long journey ahead of you.'

'But I'm staying in the house,' he protested.

'In that case we shall see quite enough of each other

tomorrow without spending the whole evening chattering,' said the Princess, turning her back on him.

'Who's that man over there?' she asked Kitty.

'Ali Montague, ma'am,' said Kitty.

'Oh, yes, I recognize the name. You can present him to me,' said Princess Margaret, heading off in Ali's direction.

The ambassador stood in consternation and silence while Kitty presented Ali Montague to Princess Margaret. He was wondering whether he was facing another diplomatic incident or merely the extension of the previous diplomatic incident.

'Oh,' said Ali Montague boldly, 'I love the French. They're treacherous, cunning, two-faced – I don't have to make an effort there, I just fit in. And further down in Italy, they're cowards as well, so I get on even better.'

The Princess looked at him mischievously. She was in a good mood again and had decided that Ali was being amusing.

Alexander Politsky later sought out Ali to congratulate him on 'handling P.M. so well'.

'Oh, I've had my fair share of royalty,' said Ali suavely. 'Mind you, I didn't do nearly so well with that dreadful Amanda Pratt. You know how ghastly all those people become when they're "on the programme" and go to all those meetings. Of course, they do save people's lives.'

Alexander sniffed and looked languidly into the middle distance. 'I've been to them myself,' he admitted.

'But you never had a drink problem,' protested Ali.

'I like heroin, cocaine, nice houses, good furniture, and pretty girls,' said Alexander, 'and I've had all of them in large quantities. But you know, they never made me happy.'

'My word, you're hard to please, aren't you?'

'Frankly, when I first went along I thought I'd stick out like a pair of jeans on a Gainsborough, but I've found more genuine love and kindness in those meetings than I've seen in all the fashionable drawing rooms of London.'

'Well, that's not saying much,' said Ali. 'You could say the same thing about Billingsgate fish market.'

'There isn't one of them,' said Alexander, throwing his shoulders back and closing his eyelids, 'from the tattooed butcher upward, whom I wouldn't drive to Inverness at three in the morning to help.'

'To Inverness? From where?' asked Ali.

'London.'

'Good God,' exclaimed Ali. 'Perhaps I should try one of those meetings, next time I have a spare evening. But the point is, would you ask your tattooed butcher to dinner?'

'Of course not,' said Alexander. 'But only because he wouldn't enjoy it.'

'Anne!' said Patrick. 'I didn't expect to see you here.'

'I know,' said Anne Eisen, kissing him warmly. 'It's not my kind of scene. I get nervous in the English countryside with everybody talking about killing animals.'

'I'm sure there isn't any of that sort of thing in Sonny's part of the world,' said Patrick.

'You mean, there isn't anything alive for miles around,' said Anne. 'I'm here because Sonny's father was a *relatively* civilized man – he noticed that there was a library in the house as well as a boot room and a cellar. He was a sort of friend of Victor's, and used to ask us to stay for weekends sometimes. Sonny was just a kid in those days but even then he was a pompous creep. Jesus,' sighed Anne, surveying the room, 'what a grim bunch. Do you think they keep them in the deep freeze at Central Casting and thaw them out for big occasions?'

'If only,' said Patrick. 'Unfortunately I think they own most of the country.'

'They've only just got the edge on an ant colony,' said Anne, 'except that they don't do anything useful. You remember those ants in Lacoste, they were always tidying up the terrace for you. Talking of doing something useful, what are you planning to do with your life?'

'Hmm,' said Patrick.

'Jesus Christ!' said Anne. 'You're guilty of the worst sin of all.'

'What's that?'

'Wasting time,' she replied.

'I know,' said Patrick. 'It was a terrible shock to me when I realized I was getting too old to die young anymore.'

Exasperated, Anne changed the subject. 'Are you going to Lacoste this year?' she asked.

'I don't know. The more time passes the more I dislike that place.'

'I've always meant to apologize to you,' said Anne, 'but you used to be too stoned to appreciate it. I've felt guilty for years for not doing anything when you were waiting on the stairs one evening during one of your parents' godawful dinner parties, and I said I'd get your mother for you, but I couldn't, and I should have gone back, or stood up to David, or something. I always felt I'd failed you.'

'Not at all,' said Patrick. 'On the contrary, I remember your being kind. When you're young it makes a difference to meet people who are kind, however rarely. You'd imagine they're buried under the routine of horror, but in fact incidents of kindness get thrown into sharp relief.'

'Have you forgiven your father?' asked Anne.

'Oddly enough you've caught me on the right evening. A week ago I would have lied or said something dismissive, but I was just describing over dinner exactly what I had to forgive my father.'

'And?'

'Well,' said Patrick, 'over dinner I was rather against forgiveness, and I still think that it's detachment rather than appeasement that will set me free, but if I could imagine a mercy that was purely human, and not one that rested on the Greatest Story Ever Told, I might extend it to my father for being so unhappy. I just can't do it out of piety. I've had enough near-death experiences to last me a lifetime, and not *once* was I greeted by a white-robed figure at the end of a tunnel – or only once and he turned out to be an exhausted junior doctor in the emergency ward of the Charing Cross Hospital. There may be something to this idea that you have to be broken in order to be renewed, but renewal doesn't have to consist of a lot of phoney reconciliations!'

'What about some genuine ones?' said Anne.

'What impresses me more than the repulsive superstition that I should turn the other cheek, is the intense unhappiness my father lived with. I ran across a diary his mother wrote during the First World War. After pages of gossip and a long passage about how marvellously they'd managed to keep up the standards at some large country house, defying the Kaiser with the perfection of their cucumber sandwiches, there are two short sentences: "Geoffrey wounded again", about her husband in the trenches, and "David has rickets", about her son at his prep school. Presumably he was not just suffering from malnutrition, but being assaulted by paedophiliac schoolmasters and beaten by older boys. This very traditional combination of maternal coldness and official perversion helped to make him the splendid man he turned into, but to forgive someone, one would have to be convinced that they'd made some effort to change the disastrous course that genetics, class, or upbringing proposed for them.'

'If he'd changed the course he wouldn't need forgiving,' said Anne. 'That's the whole deal with forgiving. Anyhow, I don't say you're wrong not to forgive him, but you can't stay stuck with this hatred.'

'There's no point in staying stuck,' Patrick agreed. 'But there's even less point in pretending to be free. I feel on the verge of a great transformation, which may be as simple as becoming interested in other things.'

'What?' said Anne. 'No more father-bashing? No more drugs? No more snobbery?'

'Steady on,' gasped Patrick. 'Mind you, this evening I had a brief hallucination that the world was real . . .'

'"An hallucination that the world was real" – you oughta be Pope.'

'Real,' Patrick continued, 'and not just composed of a series of effects – the orange lights on a wet pavement, a leaf clinging to the windscreen, the sucking sound of a taxi's tyres on a rainy street.'

'Very wintery effects,' said Anne.

'Well, it is February,' said Patrick. 'Anyway, for a moment the world seemed to be solid and out there and made up of things.'

'That's progress,' said Anne. 'You used to belong to the the-world-is-a-private-movie school.'

'You can only give things up once they start to let you down. I gave up drugs when the pleasure and the pain became simultaneous and I might as well have been shooting up a vial of my own tears. As to the naive faith that rich people are more interesting than poor ones, or titled people more interesting than untitled ones, it would be impossible to sustain if people didn't also believe that they became more interesting by association. I can feel the death throes of that particular delusion, especially as I patrol this room full of photo opportunities and feel my mind seizing up with boredom.'

'That's your own fault.'

'As to my "father-bashing",' said Patrick, ignoring Anne's comment, 'I thought of him this evening without thinking about his influence on me, just as a tired old man who'd fucked up his life, wheezing away his last years in that faded blue shirt he wore in the summer. I pictured him sitting in the courtyard of that horrible house, doing *The Times*' crossword, and he struck me as more pathetic and more *ordinary*, and in the end less worthy of attention.'

'That's what I feel about my dreadful old mother,' said Anne. 'During the Depression, which for some of us never ended, she used to collect stray cats and feed them and look after them. The house would be full of cats. I was just a kid, so naturally I'd get to love them, and play with them, but then in the autumn my crazy old mother would start muttering, "They'll never make it through the winter, they'll never make it through the winter." The only reason they weren't going to make it through the winter was that she'd soak a towel in ether and drop it in the old brass washing machine and pile the cats in afterward, and when they'd "fallen asleep" she'd turn on the washing machine and drown the poor buggers. Our whole garden was a cat cemetery, and you couldn't dig a hole or play a game without little cat skeletons turning up. There was a terrible scratching sound as they tried to get out of the washing machine. I can remember standing by the kitchen table – I was only as high as the kitchen table – while my mother loaded them in and I'd say, "Don't, please don't," and she'd be muttering, "They'll never make it through the winter." She was ghastly and quite mad, but when I grew up I figured that her worst punishment was to be herself and I didn't have to do anything more.'

'No wonder you get nervous in the English countryside when people start talking about killing animals. Perhaps that's all identity is: seeing the logic of your own experience and being true to it. If only Victor was with us now!'

'Oh, yes, poor Victor,' said Anne. 'But he was looking for a non-psychological approach to identity,' she reminded Patrick with a wry smile.

'That always puzzled me,' he admitted. 'It seemed like insisting on an overland route from England to America.'

'If you're a philosopher, there is an overland route from England to America,' said Anne.

'Oh, by the way, did you hear that George Watford had a stroke?'

'Yeah, I'm sorry to hear that. I remember meeting him at your parents.'

'It's the end of an era,' said Patrick.

'It's the end of a party as well,' said Anne. 'Look, the band is going home.'

When Robin Parker asked Sonny if they could have 'a private word' in the library, Sonny not only felt that he'd spent his entire birthday party having difficult interviews in that wretched room, but also that, as he'd suspected (and he couldn't help pausing here to congratulate himself on his perspicacity), Robin was going to blackmail him for more money.

'Well, what is it,' he said gruffly, once again sitting at his library desk.

'It isn't a Poussin,' said Robin, 'so I really don't want to authenticate it. Other people, including experts, might think it was, but I *know* it isn't.' Robin sighed. 'I'd like my letter back and of course I'll return the . . . fee,' he said, placing two thick envelopes on the table.

'What are you blathering about?' asked Sonny, confused.

'I'm not blathering,' said Robin. 'It's not fair on Poussin, that's all,' he added with unexpected passion.

'What's Poussin got to do with it?' thundered Sonny.

'Nothing, that's just what I object to.'

'I suppose you want more money.'

'You're wrong,' said Robin. 'I just want some part of my life not to be compromised.' He held out his hand for the certificate of authentication.

Furious, Sonny took a key out of his pocket and opened the top drawer of his desk, and tossed the letter over to Robin. Robin thanked him and left the room.

'Tiresome little man,' muttered Sonny. It really wasn't his day. He'd lost his wife, his mistress, and his Poussin. Buck up, old boy, he thought to himself, but he had to admit that he felt decidedly wobbly.

Virginia was sitting on a frail gold chair by the drawing-room door, waiting anxiously for her daughter and granddaughter to come downstairs and start the long drive back to Kent. Kent was ever such a long way, but she completely understood Bridget's wanting to get out of this bad atmosphere, and she'd encouraged her to bring Belinda along. She couldn't hide from herself, although she felt a little guilty about it, that she quite liked being *needed*, and having Bridget close to her again, even if it took a crisis like this one. She'd already got her overcoat and her essentials; it didn't matter about her suitcase, Bridget had said they could send for that later. She didn't want to draw attention to herself: the overcoat was suspicious enough.

The party was thinning out and it was important to leave before there were too few people, or Sonny might start badgering Bridget. Bridget's nerves had never been strong, she'd always been a little frightened as a girl, never wanted to put her head under water, that sort of thing, things only a mother could know.

Bridget might be intimidated and lose her resolve if Sonny was there booming at her, but she knew that what her daughter needed, after this Cindy Smith affair, was a good rest and a good think. She'd already asked Bridget if she wanted her old room back – it was a marvel how the human mind worked, as Roddy had been fond of remarking – but it had only seemed to annoy Bridget, who'd said, 'Honestly, Mummy, I don't know, we'll think about that later.' On reflection, it was probably better to give that room to Belinda, and put Bridget in the nice spare room with the bathroom en suite. There was plenty of room now that she was alone.

Sometimes a crisis was good for a marriage, not all the time of course, or it wouldn't really be a crisis. There'd been that one time with Roddy. She hadn't said anything, but Roddy had known she knew, and she'd known he knew she knew, and that had been enough to end it. He'd bought her that ring and said it was their second engagement ring. He was such an old softie, really. Oh dear, there was a man bearing down on her. She had no idea who he was but he was obviously going to talk to her. That was the last thing she needed.

Jacques d'Alantour was too tormented to go to

sleep and, although Jacqueline had warned him that he'd had enough to drink, too melancholy to resist another glass of champagne.

Charm was his speciality, everyone knew that, but since '*l'affaire Alantour*', as he now called it, he had entered a diplomatic labyrinth which seemed to require more charm and tact than it was reasonable to ask of a single human being. Virginia, who was, after all, his hostess's mother, played a relatively clear role in the campaign he was launching to regain Princess Margaret's favour.

'Good evening, dear lady,' he said with a deep bow.

Foreign manners, thought Virginia. What Roddy used to call 'a hand-kissing sell-your-own-mother type'.

'Am I right in assuming that you are the mother of our charming hostess?'

'Yes,' said Virginia.

'I am Jacques d'Alantour.'

'Oh, hello,' said Virginia.

'May I get you a glass of champagne?' asked the ambassador.

'No, thank you, I don't like to have more than two. Anyway, I'm on a diet.'

'A diet?' asked Monsieur d'Alantour, seeing an opportunity to prove to the world that his diplomatic skills were not dead. 'A diet?' he repeated with bewilderment and incredulity. 'But w-h-y?' he lingered on the word, to emphasize his astonishment.

'The same reason as everyone else, I suppose,' said Virginia drily.

Monsieur d'Alantour sat down next to her, grateful to get the weight off his legs. Jacqueline was right, he'd drunk too much champagne. But the campaign must continue!

'When a lady tells me she is on a diet,' he said, his gallantry a little slurred, but his fluency, from years of making the same speech (which had been a great success with the German Ambassador's wife in Paris) undiminished, 'I always clasp her breast so,' he held his cupped hand threateningly close to Virginia's alarmed bosom, 'and say, "But now I think you are exactly the right weight!" If I were to do this to you,' he continued, 'you would not be shocked, would you?'

'Shocked,' gulped Virginia, 'isn't the word. I'd be—'

'You see,' Monsieur d'Alantour interrupted, 'it's the most natural thing in the world!'

'Oh, goodness,' said Virginia, 'there's my daughter.'

'Come on, Mummy,' said Bridget, 'Belinda's already in the car, and I'd rather not run into Sonny.'

'I know, darling, I'm just coming. I can't say it's been a pleasure,' she said to the ambassador stiffly, hurrying after her daughter.

Monsieur d'Alantour was too slow to catch up with the hastening women, but stood mumbling, 'I can't express sufficiently . . . my deepest sentiments . . . a most distinguished gathering.'

Bridget moved so much faster than her guests that they had no time to compliment her or waylay her. Some thought that she was following George Watford to hospital, everyone could tell that she was on important business.

When she got into the car, a four-wheel-drive Subaru that Caroline Porlock had persuaded her to buy, and saw Belinda asleep and seatbelted in the back, and her mother sitting beside her with a warm and reassuring smile, Bridget felt a wave of relief and remorse.

'I've treated you dreadfully sometimes,' she suddenly said to her mother. 'Snobbishly.'

'Oh no, darling, I understand,' said her mother, moved but practical.

'I don't know what came over me sending you to dinner with those dreadful people. Everything gets turned upside down. I've been so anxious to fit in with Sonny's stupid, pompous life that everything else got squeezed out. Anyway, I'm glad the three of us are together.'

Virginia glanced back at Belinda to make sure she was asleep.

'We can have a good long talk tomorrow,' she said, squeezing Bridget's hand, 'but we should probably get started now, we've got a long way to go.'

'You're right,' said Bridget who suddenly felt like crying but busied herself with starting the car and joining the queue of departing guests who choked up her drive.

There was still a gentle snowfall as Patrick left the house behind him, steaming breath twisting around the upturned collar of his overcoat. Footprints criss-crossed his path, and the gravel's black and brown chips shone wetly among the bright patches of snow. Patrick's ears rang from the noise of the party and his eyes, bloodshot from smoke and tiredness, watered in the cold air, but when he reached his car he wanted to go on walking a little longer, and so he climbed over a nearby gate and jumped into a field of unbroken snow. A pewter-coloured ornamental lake lay at the end of the field, its far bank lost in a thick fog.

His thin shoes grew wet as he crunched across the field and his feet soon felt cold, but with the compelling and opaque logic of a dream the lake drew him to its shore.

As he stood in front of the reeds which pierced the first few yards of water, shivering and wondering whether to have his last cigarette, he heard the sound of beating wings emerging from the other side of the lake. A pair of swans rose out of the fog, concentrating its whiteness and giving it shape, the clamour of their wings muffled by the falling snow, like white gloves on applauding hands.

Vicious creatures, thought Patrick.

The swans, indifferent to his thoughts, flew over fields renewed and silenced by the snow, curved back over the shore of the lake, spread their webbed feet, and settled confidently onto the water.

Standing in sodden shoes Patrick smoked his last cigarette. Despite his tiredness and the absolute stillness of the air, he felt his soul, which he could only characterize as the part of his mind that was not dominated by the need to talk, surging and writhing like a kite longing to be let go. Without thinking about it he picked up the dead branch at his feet and sent it spinning as far as he could into the dull grey eye of the lake. A faint ripple disturbed the reeds.

After their useless journey the swans drifted majestically back into the fog. Nearer and noisier, a group of gulls circled overhead, their squawks evoking wilder water and wider shores.

Patrick flicked his cigarette into the snow, and not quite knowing what had happened, headed back to his car with a strange feeling of elation.